WEB OF LIES

Virginia Smith

AnniesFiction.com

Books in the Sweet Intrigue series

. . . and more to come!

Library of Congress-in-Publication Data
Web of Lies / by Virginia Smith
p. cm.
I. Title
                        2020952149

AnniesFiction.com
(800) 282-6643
Annie's Sweet Intrigue™
Series Creator: Shari Lohner
Editor: Lorie Jones

10 11 12 13 14 | Printed in South Korea | 9 8 7 6 5 4 3 2 1

A scorching tension had settled in the conference room at Skytech 1 Industries, rendering the air nearly unbreathable.

Shifting uncomfortably in her chair, Brooke Lester glanced at the five members of her department seated around the oval table. They fiddled with their phones, tapped notes on their tablets, or simply stared at the polished surface directly in front of them. No one could meet Ed Gentry's blistering gaze from the head of the table.

"Well?" Ed asked, his voice filling the room like the bellow of a bear. "Isn't there one person in this department with brains enough to figure out what happened?"

Brooke tried to catch her boss's eye across the table. But Jordan Lancaster focused on his notebook—the old-fashioned paper kind he favored, which Brooke found humorous for the assistant director of a technology company—and rolled a pen absently between his fingers. Deep creases marred his forehead, and he chewed on his lower lip in the distracted way that meant he was deep in thought.

"You're in charge of this project," Ed growled, turning his wrath on Jordan. "Do you want to tell me why the system crashed today?"

Meeting Ed's gaze, Jordan drew in a long breath before answering in a calm voice. "We don't know yet. We're analyzing the data now."

Brooke had no idea how Jordan managed to maintain his composure while being berated.

Jordan held the man's gaze and continued evenly. "Or we would be, if the entire team weren't sitting in this meeting."

Brooke lowered her head to hide a smile. Nobody but Jordan had the nerve to speak up to the volatile director of research and development.

Blood suffused Ed's cheeks, and he launched himself out of the chair, snorting like an angry bull. "Listen to me. In the past three years, we have sunk millions of dollars into this new technology. This storage array is supposed to be ready for beta testing in two weeks. We are going to revolutionize the data storage industry with this product, and that will put us in a position to monopolize the global market."

The room was eerily silent.

Ed planted his fists on the table and leaned over them, glowering. "We will have a ten-drive stripe storage array ready to show the shareholders by September 30, or there won't be a single person in this room who still has a job on October 1. Do I make myself clear?"

When the director glanced in her direction, Brooke fought the impulse to scoot down in the leather chair. Instead, she held herself erect and met his eye.

Ed's expression didn't change as his gaze flickered over her without stopping. Though she couldn't help but notice he spared a curt nod for Greg Flynn and another for Derek Ingram, the two systems programmers from MIT, Ed's alma mater.

"Good." Ed straightened, then pointed at Jordan. "I expect an e-mail waiting for me when I get here tomorrow morning, telling me exactly what went wrong and how you've corrected the issue."

Jordan dipped his head forward in a silent acknowledgment.

Apparently satisfied that he'd sufficiently roused the team to action, Ed marched out of the conference room.

The tension dissipated, and everyone drew a collective sigh.

A tired smile settled on Jordan's lips. "I guess we all know what we'll be doing tonight."

A couple of people groaned.

"Derek and Brooke, I want you to double-check those test scripts," Jordan continued. "Larry, you and Roger analyze the operating system schematics. Greg, you and I will comb through the application code. Feel free to work from home if you need to, but I'd like an e-mailed summary from each of you by 5:00 a.m." He strode from the room.

Across the table from Brooke, Roger gave a dramatic sigh. "I'll have to cancel a date with the woman who might turn out to be the future Mrs. Roger Kirk."

Beside him, Greg twisted in his chair. "I haven't heard you mention anyone special."

Roger picked up his tablet and heaved himself to his feet. "I haven't actually met her in person yet. But you should see her online dating profile." He gave a long wolf whistle.

His three male coworkers laughed.

Roger flashed an apologetic smile at Brooke. "Sorry. What I mean is, she's really smart."

Brooke managed not to snort while she collected her own tablet and cell phone. Roger was a brilliant programmer, but she privately referred to him as Romeo Roger. He considered himself a ladies' man. In the six months she'd worked for the company, she couldn't count the number of blind dates he'd had, but she could tick off the number of second dates on her fingers and have a few to spare. Apparently he wasn't quite the Don Juan he thought himself.

On her way out of the conference room, Derek caught up with her. The MIT grad stood several inches taller and carried himself with a cocky confidence that always seemed to border on condescension. At least he spoke to her, the lone female in the R & D department.

"I'll be working from home," Derek said, sneering down a well-shaped nose at her. "You can send me your write-up, and I'll summarize our report for Jordan."

Right. And take credit for my work. Brooke pasted on a pleasant smile. "Sure, I'll do that." *And I'll make sure to copy Jordan on anything I send you.*

Derek started to leave, then stopped short. A frown darkened his features.

Curious, Brooke followed his gaze across the maze of chest-high cubicles in the R & D department. On the other side of the room stood Ed. His arm was casually draped across the corner of Greg's cubicle. Ed's rage from the conference room was gone, replaced by a smile. Greg stood in front of him, the two conversing in a friendly manner. He said something, and Ed threw back his head and laughed.

Derek's jaw tightened. Though Derek and Greg both hailed from MIT, they weren't friends. They'd joined the storage array project a few months apart from each other, shortly after the project's inception. The two maintained a fierce competition, especially when it came to gaining the director's approval.

Derek stalked toward them, determination in every line of his body.

Shaking her head, Brooke headed toward Jordan's office in the opposite direction. She'd learned months ago that it wouldn't do any good to try to curry favor with Ed. He apparently viewed the department's only female systems engineer as unworthy of his attention.

At first she'd fretted over the fact that he never spoke to her outside of meetings or congratulated her on accomplishments. Ed's slight was especially noticeable because Jordan freely praised a job well done and genuinely appreciated the efforts of everyone on his team, regardless of gender. Brooke had finally decided not to waste her efforts on Ed. At least she hadn't been asked to fetch his coffee. Yet.

Management employees at the company enjoyed the luxury of real walls and a door that closed, though Jordan's door almost always stood open as it was now. Inside, he sat at his desk, tapping on his keyboard, his intent gaze fixed on the monitor.

Brooke paused in the doorway and waited for him to notice her. When he didn't, she cleared her throat.

Jordan raised his head, though he didn't take his hands from the keyboard. "Oh, hi. Do you need something?"

"I was wondering if you'd had time to go over the prototype model I sent the other day."

His features remained blank for a long moment. "No, I haven't. I'm sorry. I've had a million other things going on, and then today happened." He cast a grimace toward the conference room. "Figuring out what compromised the system this morning has to take top priority." His gaze strayed back to the monitor. "But as soon as we get that glitch nailed down, I'll go over your prototype."

Clearly, Jordan was engrossed in whatever he was doing. Probably examining code, trying to find the needle that blew up their haystack.

A guilty flush warmed her neck. She should be doing the same instead of wasting his time on a different project. "Of course," she said, taking a step backward. "Whenever."

Jordan gave an absent nod, his fingers already flying over the keyboard.

As Brooke returned to her own cubicle, her stomach rumbled. A glance at her fitness tracker announced the reason. After seven o'clock already? And she had several hours' work ahead of her. She opened her drawer and inspected her stash of protein bars. Nothing tempted her. But ordering a pizza and working from home in her PJs sounded like a plan she could get behind.

Sliding into her desk chair, she attached today's test script files to an e-mail and sent it off to her personal account, then grabbed her purse.

As Brooke strode through the department, she noticed that Ed was gone and Derek and Greg were locked in a heated discussion.

She quickened her pace and escaped out the door.

The large newsroom buzzed with an energy akin to a kindergarten class charged with a steady diet of jelly beans. Even now, with the sun nothing more than a faint line on the Pacific horizon, journalists worked at a frantic pace, their fingers pounding out headlines that would grab the public by the throat. The sounds in the cavernous room combined to form a bedlam-like din that made concentration impossible. The smell of coffee—so strong that it stung Connor Dyson's nostrils—permeated the room. He didn't want to consider whether it was from the coffee station in the corner or the breath of a hundred journalists.

Once Connor had thrived on this kind of intensity. Five years ago, when he'd landed this gig as a beat reporter in Los Angeles, he'd felt like the proverbial small-town Ohio kid who'd wandered into the press box of a Cincinnati Reds baseball game. There was something interesting to see everywhere he looked. Now he had a hard time filtering out the racket. These days he did his best work at home in the silence of his loft apartment.

Not that he had anything exciting to write about. His beat, the area of news to which he'd been assigned, was local business. And not the big businesses either. The subjects of Connor's articles were family-owned restaurants in danger of closing because a customer contracted food poisoning from the chicken fingers. Or retail stores that offered giant weekend sales. How could a guy be expected to write compelling copy about inconsequential retail garbage in the midst of a cacophony of competing journalists shouting about their breaking news? No, it took concentration best found in solitude to make the half-off sale at Sandford's Surf Shop sound important.

Maybe he should reconsider his parents' persistent suggestion that he return to Ohio and take a job at the local newspaper. There he would be a big fish in a tiny pond. Whereas here . . .

He glanced around the newsroom, crowded with desks and bursting with activity. Here he was a guppy in an ocean.

Shaking his head, Connor shut down his computer, locked his desk drawers—his coworkers were mostly trustworthy, but they were still curious reporters—and slid his cell phone into the side pocket of his jeans.

"Dyson!" came a shout from the far corner of the room. "Got a minute?"

Connor located the source. Steven Fitzsimmons, known as Fitz to one and all, gestured at him from the doorway of his glass-enclosed office.

"Sure." Connor rolled his chair neatly beneath his desk and headed toward the deputy managing editor's office.

"Got an anonymous tip on the hotline that something significant is happening soon over at Skytech 1 Industries," Fitz said when he approached. "Maybe a layoff. Think you could swing by there in the morning and sniff around?"

Connor straightened, his investigative instinct on high alert. Skytech 1 wasn't a local retail company, like he was generally assigned. A story about an international technology firm could lead to something big. It might give him the opportunity to work on more-exciting assignments that would get him noticed.

He adopted an air of nonchalance and actually shrugged. "Yeah. Got a contact?"

Fitz heaved a laugh. "You wish. Anonymous call. Just go see what you can find out. The woman in charge of media relations is a good place to start." He frowned. "Her name's Muffin."

Connor raised his eyebrows. "Ms. Muffin? Are you sure about that?"

"Mumford. Mufworth. Something like that." Fitz waved a hand in dismissal. "Research it yourself."

When the editor retreated into his office, Connor crossed the crowded newsroom and headed for the door. Skytech 1 was a public corporation, so their directory would be posted on their website. That was the first thing he'd check out. But he wouldn't stop there.

By the time he arrived at the company's headquarters tomorrow, he'd know everything there was to know about Skytech 1 Industries.

Brooke stifled a yawn as she parked her car in the employee lot at Skytech 1 Industries the next morning. It was a quarter after seven, a little later than she normally came to the office, but she still had almost two hours before work officially started at nine.

Of course, this morning the R & D team might be even later than usual, since they'd all worked into the wee hours trying to pinpoint the cause of yesterday's test failure. She had sent her summary e-mail to Jordan at almost three o'clock, reporting that she had found exactly nothing. Whatever had caused the storage array to fail, it wasn't a faulty test script.

As Brooke walked to the security door on the side of the building, she realized that she wasn't the first person to arrive. Jordan's and Ed's cars were both already in the parking lot. Ed was an early bird like her, but Jordan didn't typically arrive until close to nine. He must have come in early because of the test failure.

She used her employee badge to unlock the door, then entered the building. The office lay in darkness except for the emergency lights along the far wall. Why hadn't Jordan turned on the lights? She flicked a switch, and fluorescent light illuminated the maze of cubicles.

On the way to her desk, Brooke stopped in the break room and started a pot of coffee. She smiled. No amount of money could entice her to make coffee during the day, lest she be stereotyped. But first thing in the morning? And especially after three hours' sleep? Coffee was required.

After the coffee brewed, she poured herself a cup, then strode to her cubicle and stowed her purse in the drawer.

The muffled sound of a ringing phone reached her as she flipped on her computer. Glancing around, she located the source. Jordan's office. The door was shut. And he clearly wasn't inside, because no light shone around the edges of the doorframe. Maybe he was upstairs in Ed's office, delivering the update in person. Hopefully someone had found the problem.

The ringing persisted until the call went to voice mail. Then Jordan's phone rang again.

Brooke wondered who would be calling the office so early. Whoever it was, they were certainly persistent. That call also went to voice mail.

Her monitor remained black. What was wrong with her computer? She pressed the button again, but nothing happened.

She couldn't believe that something was wrong with her computer today of all days, when they had to start working on a new test. Now she was going to have to call tech support, and it would probably take them hours to figure out—

The phone on her desk rang. Frowning, Brooke glanced at the digital screen. An unfamiliar number with a Los Angeles area code. She snatched up the receiver. "R & D, Brooke Lester."

"Good morning," a pleasant female voice said. "This is Holly Lancaster."

Holly was Jordan's wife. Brooke had met her a few times when she dropped by the office. "What can I do for you?" Brooke asked.

"I took a chance you'd be there," Holly said. "Jordan tells me you're always the first one at work."

The thought brought a smile to Brooke's lips. The boss not only noticed her efforts, but he had even commented to his wife about her.

"Jordan isn't answering his cell phone or his office phone," Holly continued. "I'm wondering if he's in his office."

Brooke glanced at the closed office door. "No, his office is dark. He must be upstairs talking to Ed."

"You're probably right," Holly said. She sounded unconcerned. "He left the house a couple of hours ago to stop at the gym because he had an early meeting at the office. I hate to ask, but could you put a message on his desk?" She gave an apologetic laugh. "I've left a voice message, but sometimes he doesn't check those for hours. And his cell is off because it doesn't even ring before it goes to voice mail."

"Sure." Brooke pulled a pad of sticky notes toward her and grabbed a pen. "What do you want to say?"

"Tell him not to forget Aria's one-year checkup this morning at eleven," Holly answered.

"He's supposed to meet me at the doctor's office. He's been so stressed with work the past few days, and I'm afraid it will slip his mind."

Brooke jotted down the reminder. "I know he'd hate to miss that." Jordan adored his daughter, which was evident to anyone who'd ever walked into his office and had seen the dozens of photographs of her. She peeled the note off the pad. "Consider him reminded."

"Thanks so much," Holly said. "I appreciate it."

They ended the call.

Brooke headed for Jordan's office. She started to stick the note on the door but hesitated. A yellow square on a door was an invitation for nosy coworkers. She decided it was better to put the note on his desk instead.

She twisted the knob and reached inside to flip the switch. The room lit up, and she froze in horror.

The office was in disarray. Papers littered the floor and the surface of the desk. An empty trash can was on its side near the guest chair. A lamp had been overturned and now rested broken on the floor. What in the world had happened in here? She took a step, and something crunched beneath her foot. Glass? She bent down and picked up a picture frame. Aria's smiling baby face beamed at her, the photo scratched by shattered glass.

Then she noticed Jordan. He lay partially hidden on the floor behind his desk. His dark eyes fixed on a sight no one else would ever see. A black cord had been looped around his neck.

It took Brooke a moment to process what she was seeing. When she did, her hand flew to her mouth to stifle a scream.

Jordan was dead.

A little after eight o'clock on Thursday morning, Connor took the off-ramp from the highway toward Skytech 1 Industries. A notebook on the seat beside him contained several pages of his scrawled handwriting, notes from last night's research. He intended to be waiting for Ms. Marcella Mullins, vice president of media relations, when she arrived for work.

He joined a line of cars flooding into the parking lot, then stomped on the brakes when the SUV in front of him came to a sudden stop. The reason was immediately apparent. A row of police cars, lights flashing, blocked the parking spaces nearest the building. A handful of uniformed officers stood in front of them, directing the new arrivals to the right or left like parking attendants at a theme park.

Connor felt a rush of excitement, and he tightened his grip on the steering wheel. Something unusual was going on, something big. And he was here to see it.

He pulled out of the line and sped toward an empty spot at the far end of the lot. From this vantage point, he spied an ambulance backed up to the edge of a set of stairs leading to the building's entryway. Snatching his notebook, he exited his Mustang and hurried down the length of the building toward the main entrance.

Skytech 1 Industries occupied a long building, the majority of which was dedicated to the manufacturing plant. The administrative offices were located at the north end, and a crowd had gathered there, held at bay by two uniformed police officers. Men and women in casual business attire stood before them in loose knots, whispering to one another.

Connor joined the closest group. "What's going on?"

A man shrugged. "No idea. They won't tell us anything."

The woman standing next to him stared intently at the closed entrance doors, her brow a field of worried creases. "I hope there hasn't been an accident." She turned to her coworker. "You know, an industrial accident of some sort."

The man's lips twisted with disdain. "We don't deal in hazardous materials, if that's what you mean."

"I know that," she said, stiffening. "But accidents can happen around machinery."

"Then the police would be down at the plant entrance," he reasoned. "Not here."

Connor left the two people to speculate and headed toward the front of the crowd. He made his way right up to where the police kept people behind an invisible line. Journalistic senses on high alert, he studied the people around him, searching for anyone with an air of importance. Two men, both wearing ties, stood off to one side, talking quietly to each other. They appeared to be a couple of bosses, but they seemed as clueless as everyone else.

A woman emerged from the crowd and raced toward the police officers.

Connor pushed closer.

The woman displayed an ID badge and said something too low to be overheard.

The officer stepped aside to let her approach the building.

"Marcella!" a man shouted.

Connor's ears perked up. Marcella Mullins, the very woman he'd come here to see.

She halted and faced the executive who'd called her.

"What's going on?" the man demanded.

Marcella held a palm toward him. "Michael will give a statement soon, Gary. Just hang tight out here." Then she trotted up the stairs. When she reached the entrance, someone opened the door from the inside, and she disappeared through it.

Connor inspected Gary. The man's scowl proved that he was not accustomed to being told to "hang tight." Connor conjured the mental list of executives he'd found on the company's website. Gary Chambers was the vice president of finance. Whatever was going on inside was big enough that the VP of media relations was called in while some of the company's top executives weren't. Connor's mind raced with possibilities.

He pulled out his cell phone and tapped a text to Fitz. *Something's up at Skytech 1. Police. Ambulance. Building closed to employees.*

His boss replied barely five seconds later. *Get the scoop. And pics.*

Of course. Why hadn't he been taking pictures? Connor aimed his cell phone at the building, making sure to get the officers in the foreground, and snapped. He took a shot of the crowd and one of the ambulance, its doors standing open and ready for . . . what? He didn't know, but he wasn't about to miss it.

The doors opened again, and a woman in a different uniform appeared. An EMT. She pulled a stretcher behind her.

A gasp went up from the crowd, and someone pressed against Connor's back as the onlookers surged forward.

"Everybody," one of the police officers said in a loud voice, "please stay back."

Four EMTs wheeled the stretcher through the doorway and transported it down the concrete stairs, their expressions solemn. And no wonder. The figure they carried was covered head to toe in a white sheet.

Connor continued to snap pictures on his cell phone, dimly aware that others around him were doing the same.

Straps held the body—it was impossible to tell whether it was male or female—in place as the EMTs approached the ambulance and unlocked the trolley's axle. The frame folded, and they slid their burden into the back of the vehicle.

Soft sobs sounded from someone behind him as the police officers cleared a path through the crowd for the ambulance to exit the parking lot.

The moment the ambulance pulled out of sight, the doors to the building opened. A man clad in casual clothing appeared, followed by Marcella Mullins and a third man dressed in a suit.

Immediately the two executives who were already on the scene strode forward, their body language announcing to one and all that they would not "hold tight" a moment longer.

"Michael, what's going on?" Gary demanded.

Michael Harmon, whom Connor now recognized from his research as the CEO of Skytech 1 Industries, raked his fingers through his hair, then lifted his head to speak to the crowd. "There's been an—" He stopped and glanced at Marcella, who whispered something to him. "An incident. A very sad incident."

"Who was that?" someone asked in a trembling voice.

Mr. Harmon shook his head. "I'm afraid I can't tell you, not until the next of kin has been notified. But the office will be closed today. We'll have a company-wide meeting tomorrow, and I'll tell you what I know then."

Now several people were openly crying.

Marcella touched the CEO on the sleeve, then nodded over the heads of the crowd.

Connor followed her gaze and saw two television news vans zoom into the parking lot. Frustrated, he gritted his teeth. No way was he going to get scooped by the broadcast media. He flipped his phone camera to video and pointed it at Mr. Harmon.

"I'd like the executive team to come inside," Mr. Harmon said. "The rest of you can go home for the rest of the day." Extreme sadness washed over his features, and he continued in a choked voice. "There's a family who is about to get some tragic news. Please say a prayer for them."

Several people moved toward him, and others started walking away.

Flanked by a handful of people, Mr. Harmon disappeared inside the building, leaving Marcella behind.

She addressed the group. "The media is arriving now, and no doubt they'll have questions, as we all do. Please don't speculate on anything you've seen or heard this morning. We will make an official announcement as soon as we're able."

"Why can't you tell us what's going on now?" a man asked. Anger rumbled in his voice.

Marcella searched the crowd and motioned to a man. "Would you like to find out on the morning news that your wife had died?"

The man's eyes widened, and he didn't respond.

"That's why we can't tell you now. I'll see you tomorrow." Marcella slipped through the doors.

The first of the news vans screeched to a halt.

Connor stopped the recording on his phone and allowed himself to be ushered away from the building by the attending officers.

A couple of local news anchors hopped out of the vehicles and began circulating through the crowd, trying to pry information from people who knew nothing. Most of the employees made their way to their cars, and engines started all over the parking lot.

Connor stopped on the sidewalk a little apart from the commotion and studied the area. At the front of the lot was a row of reserved parking places. Those were closest to the building's entrance, probably for executives. Only two spaces were occupied, by a BMW and a Lexus. The rest remained empty. Beyond them, in the first space that wasn't reserved, stood a blue Toyota. The entire rest of the row was vacant, blocked off by the police. Obviously the blue compact had arrived before the police. An early employee?

The rest of the crowd moved away from the building, and no one approached the blue car. He wondered if it was because the driver was still inside the building—or maybe inside the ambulance.

Connor left the sidewalk. Skirting most of the crowd and avoiding the news reporters, he approached the Toyota from the rear. He took a picture of the license plate before heading to his own vehicle to wait.

He had all the time in the world to find out what had happened.

Though the contents had long since gone cold, Brooke continued to clutch her mug in both hands. Her trembling had finally stopped, thanks in part to the bracing coffee someone had poured for her and the jacket one of the female police officers had thrown around her shoulders.

Brooke stood at the corner of her cubicle, watching through the open door of Jordan's office as an officer wearing rubber gloves boxed up his belongings. She shuddered when she remembered stepping on shards of glass and finding the scratched picture of Jordan's precious daughter, Aria, on the floor.

Jordan was dead. Her numb brain had a hard time grasping the reality. Her boss was dead and not of natural causes. The chaos in the office—the broken lamp, shattered glass, and scattered papers—was evidence of a struggle. Someone had killed him.

Activity at the other end of the long room drew her attention. Mr. Harmon returned, along with several of the company's executives.

A powerfully built man with short dark hair stopped the group's progress and spoke in a low voice.

After the brief conversation, most of the group retreated down the hallway toward the elevators. Their expressions showed emotions ranging from concern to irritation.

Mr. Harmon headed in Brooke's direction with the dark-haired man at his side.

"How are you holding up?" the CEO asked, his tone sympathetic.

She drew a shaky breath. "Okay, I guess. It was quite a shock."

It was a mild description of the deep horror that still racked her insides. Would she ever be able to erase the horrible sight of Jordan's corpse from her memory? She'd never seen a dead person outside of a funeral. He'd looked so unnatural. So horrible.

"I'm sure it was." Sympathy colored Mr. Harmon's tone. "This is Detective Jason Travis. As soon as he says it's okay, I want you to go home and try to relax. Take a few days off."

Brooke glanced at the detective, whose expression held the sympathy of a stone, and turned back to Mr. Harmon. "Has Holly been told yet?"

Sadness pulled at his features. "Leanne and a police officer are at her house now."

Leanne, one of the managers in the human resources department, was known for her compassion and her gentle manner. One part of Brooke's mind acknowledged the wisdom of sending Leanne with the police, but the other part snagged on something else Mr. Harmon said. She wasn't free to leave until Detective Travis gave his permission?

Brooke eyed Travis cautiously. "I've already told the other officer everything I know. I'm not sure what else I can do here."

"If you don't mind, I'd like to hear your statement firsthand." Not even a hint of a smile disturbed the detective's rigidly held mouth.

Mr. Harmon rested a sympathetic hand on her shoulder. "I understand you've been through a lot, but I appreciate whatever you can do to help them figure out what happened."

Brooke nodded. Of course she wanted to provide whatever assistance she could.

"Thank you." Mr. Harmon patted her shoulder. "Excuse me. I need to go upstairs with the executive committee and start notifying the board of directors." He retreated, leaving her alone with the detective.

Travis scanned the area. "Is there somewhere we can talk in private?"

Though she wasn't at all sure she wanted to be alone with him, she pointed at a closed door. "The conference room is over there."

"Great." He gestured for her to lead the way, calling, "Lewis!"

To Brooke's relief, the female officer who'd given her the jacket broke away from a cluster of her coworkers and joined them. Something about Travis's rigid manner made her uneasy, defensive even. She hoped having another woman in the room would help put her at ease.

The relief proved to be temporary. When they entered the conference room, Brooke sat in the chair she typically occupied for department meetings. Travis circled the table and took a seat directly across from her. Instead of joining them, Officer Lewis shut the door and stood in the corner beside it, just behind Brooke but still visible in her peripheral vision. She stood stiffly and seemed intent on mirroring the detective's lack of emotion.

Travis folded his hands and rested them on the table in front of him. "Now, tell me what happened."

Forcing herself to speak calmly, Brooke detailed her steps from the moment she'd arrived at work until she entered Jordan's office.

"And then you called Mr. Gentry," the detective said.

"That's right."

"Why did you call him?" he asked, removing a notepad and a pen from his pocket.

"I saw his car in the parking lot, so I knew he was here."

"Yes, but why didn't you call 911?" Travis asked. "Surely that would be the appropriate thing to do in an emergency situation."

From the corner of her eye, Brooke glimpsed Officer Lewis lean slightly forward, as if waiting to hear the answer.

"Ed is the director and Jordan's boss." Brooke's thoughts raced. Why hadn't she dialed 911? The idea had never crossed her mind. "I guess I didn't think of calling for help because it was obvious he was, well, already dead." The explanation sounded lame, even to her.

"I see." Travis's stony expression changed as one corner of his mouth twitched in an acerbic smirk. "It didn't occur to you that the killer might still be in the building and that you might be in danger?"

Brooke jerked back in the seat. Her skin crawled as she pictured the murderer hiding in the office. Had the killer seen her? "I never thought of that."

The detective's smirk deepened before vanishing. "Let's back up a bit. You say you didn't enter the building through the main doors, but you came in the side."

Brooke drew a shuddering breath to center herself. "Yes, that's right. That's the door I always use."

Travis jotted down notes, then looked at her. "Why?"

Still shaken, she gaped at him. He seemed intent on making her defend every single action. "Because it's the closest door to where I park my car."

"I noticed the main entrance is monitored by security cameras," he said. "Is the side door monitored as well?"

Was he accusing her of trying to sneak inside without anyone seeing her? A flicker of anger made her clench her fists beneath the conference table. He was treating her as if she'd done something wrong.

"Why don't you ask Ed what he saw?" Brooke suggested. "His car was in the parking lot when I got here. He must have heard something."

"We've spoken with Mr. Gentry," the detective said. "He arrived a few minutes after seven, and he heard nothing. Security records verify his time of arrival." He tapped his notepad. "Please answer the question. Is the side door monitored by cameras?"

"Yes, and it's secured as well," she answered with a note of defiance. "I used my employee badge to get in, like I always do. You can check with the security department. I'm sure they have records."

"Don't worry. We will." Travis rocked back in the chair, cocked his head, and studied her for a long moment.

With an effort, Brooke managed not to squirm under the intense scrutiny and returned his stare without blinking. She imagined this was what it must feel like to be a bug under a microscope.

When the silence had stretched long enough to be uncomfortable, she asked, "Is there anything else? I've had a really bad morning, and I'd like to go home."

A smile hovered around his thin lips. "In time," he responded. "Tell me, were you and Mr. Lancaster friends?"

The question took her aback. "We weren't exactly friends. I mean, he was my boss."

Travis raised his eyebrows. "So you disliked him?"

The reality of the situation struck Brooke, making her head spin. The detective's probing questions and accusing manner had a sinister purpose. He was trying to get a confession out of her.

The police believed she was a murderer.

"I've told you everything I know." Brooke tried to pitch her voice in a calm tone, but the last forty minutes trapped in the conference room with Detective Travis were wearing on her. And trapped was exactly what was going on. He was trying to trap her by repeating the same questions, phrased a little differently each time. "Several times."

Should she refuse to say anything else without an attorney present? That was what people did on television. But usually those people turned out to be guilty, and she didn't want to give the impression that she was guilty or uncooperative. Besides, she didn't know any attorneys.

"Let's go back to Mrs. Lancaster's phone call." Travis sat with his elbows planted on the table, his fingers steepled and tapping against each other. "You say she called his office phone twice and then called you. Why you?"

Brooke bit back a sigh. "She said Jordan had told her I was always in the office early," she repeated for at least the third time.

"It's interesting that Mr. Lancaster would discuss the work habits of his employees with his wife," he remarked. "I wonder if he told her anything else about you."

Caution crept over Brooke. Where was he going with that statement? "You'd have to ask her about that," she said carefully.

"Yes, I will," the detective said. "But I'm curious about your thoughts. Would Mrs. Lancaster have any reason to be jealous of your *friendship* with her husband?"

Heat flooded Brooke's cheeks. The sudden rush of blood brought with it a moment of clarity. She was being manipulated. Travis had no doubt been trained in interrogation techniques, ways to catch people off guard so they would say something to incriminate themselves. Only that wouldn't work with her because she had done nothing wrong.

Brooke leaned forward in her chair and held the detective's gaze. "That. Is. Insulting," she told him, her words staccato. "If you're trying to get a reaction out of me with baseless and offensive insinuations, then obviously you have no valid questions left to ask and this interview is over."

He studied her for a long moment, during which Brooke concentrated on keeping her posture rigid and her breath even.

Finally, Travis nodded. "I think that's enough for now," he said almost pleasantly. "You may go." He remained seated.

Brooke got stiffly to her feet. She held her head high as she swept past Officer Lewis and jerked the door open.

Travis's voice stopped her. "Ms. Lester."

She halted.

"Don't try to leave town."

There it was. An acknowledgment that she was indeed a suspect. Her heart pounding, she left without looking back.

Connor remained at Skytech 1, waiting for something to happen. The mood in the parking lot was expectant and tense.

Most of the employees had left, but a small group of them remained. The vice president of media relations had promised to make an official announcement, and the stragglers seemed determined to stay until they'd heard what Marcella had to say. All but two of the police officers had also left, and the two remaining stood immediately outside the building's entrance, talking quietly and continuing to keep others out of the building. The television reporters had given up trying to question the onlookers and hovered on the sidelines, but they appeared ready to spring into action at the first sign of activity.

Connor sat in his Mustang with the windows down, his ears tuned to catch the occasional snatch of conversation. He'd texted all the pictures and video he'd taken to Fitz, including the one of the blue Toyota's license plate. Hopefully he'd learn the owner's identity soon.

A sudden buzz of voices drew his attention to the front of the building, where one of the doors had opened. The officers stepped aside as a young brunette woman emerged. She was tall but slightly built, and she clutched a colorful quilted purse with both hands.

The reporters rushed toward her, thrusting their microphones in her direction.

Ignoring the reporters and the questions from her fellow coworkers in the crowd, the woman hurried down the walkway with her head down.

Connor aimed his cell phone and took several pictures of her as she made a beeline for the blue compact. Something stirred in him at the sight of her hunched shoulders and the way her hair fell in a thick curtain to obscure her identity.

Voices called to her, and he heard several shouts of "Brooke! What's going on?"

A male reporter planted himself in her path and reached out a hand to physically stop her.

Connor grabbed his door handle, ready to leap out of the car and come to her aid.

But she sidestepped the reporter and broke into a brisk trot. When she arrived at her car and fumbled in her purse, he lost sight of her as the people pressed around her. A moment later, the engine rumbled to life, and the Toyota rolled backward.

People jumped out of the way.

Connor got a good picture of the woman as the car sped past him toward the exit.

His phone beeped, announcing the arrival of a text.

He checked the screen. Fitz had sent him the mystery woman's name and address.

The reporters now had a new line of questioning and began circulating through the crowd, no doubt asking the questions Connor would ask himself. Who was that woman? What did they know about her?

Well, Connor knew that her name was Brooke Lester, and he also knew where she lived. He punched the address into his GPS app, started his car, and zoomed after the Toyota.

Twenty minutes later, he turned onto a residential street in a decent neighborhood. Cars lined both sides, parked in front of small, nearly identical houses. Up ahead he caught a glimpse of blue and watched as the Toyota came to a stop in a driveway. He slowed, scanning the street for an empty parking place, and spied one on his right. Whipping his vehicle into it, he exited the car in time to see her disappear into the house.

Connor jogged up the short sidewalk and knocked on the door. No response.

He knocked again. "Ms. Lester, I'd like to speak with you if you don't mind. It'll only take a minute."

The door opened a crack. A tearstained face, nose reddened and lids puffy above a pair of sea-green eyes, appeared. "Are you with the police?"

"No, I'm not." If he identified himself as a journalist, she probably wouldn't talk to him. "My name is Connor Dyson. Can you tell me what happened this morning at Skytech 1 Industries?"

"I've already told the police everything I know," Brooke said, then started to shut the door.

He put a hand on the door. What question could he ask that wouldn't get her guard up? "How well did you know the deceased?"

Her throat bobbed, and a sob escaped her. "Jordan is—*was* my boss."

Jordan wasn't a name he recognized from the corporate website, so he must not have been one of the top executives.

"I'm so sorry for your loss." Connor poured sympathy into his voice and not merely as an act. The sight of her grief tightened his chest.

Brooke sniffled. "Thank you."

He cast about for another query that would give him a lead, something to follow up on. "Were you with him when it happened?"

Apparently that was the wrong question to ask. Her posture became stiff, her tone suspicious. "Who are you?"

"Connor Dyson." He displayed what he hoped was a sympathetic smile. "I simply want to know what happened."

"How did you find me? Did you follow me?"

"No," he rushed to say. Honesty was his best approach. "I'm a newspaper journalist. I ran your license plate."

She sucked in a breath, her anger apparent. "How dare you! Go away and don't come back." Her lips twisted. "Or I'll give your name to a very nasty police detective."

Connor jumped back just in time to avoid having his nose broken by the slamming door.

Brooke sat on the sofa in her small living room, her feet tucked beneath her and Sammy the Siamese curled in her lap. The cat drowsed, a contented purr rumbling in his chest as Brooke absently stroked his back.

She had adopted Sammy from a local animal shelter, and he had been her constant companion since she moved into this rental house. Brooke needed the cat's comforting presence now more than ever.

On the other side of the room, the television screen showed the exterior of the building where she'd spent the majority of her time for the past six months. Across the bottom ran a banner announcing this was breaking news. A female reporter—one she recognized from the crowd outside the building an hour ago—spoke into a microphone, though Brooke had lowered the volume. She didn't care to hear the speculations of the newspeople.

The woman peered at something off to the side, and then the camera focused on the front entrance of Skytech 1 Industries. Mr. Harmon exited the building, followed by the members of the executive team. The CEO stopped at the top of the stairs, and the others formed a line behind him. Detective Travis arrived to stand at Mr. Harmon's right, folded his arms across his chest, and scowled at the camera.

A shudder shook Brooke's frame, and she battled a rush of dislike. In the next moment, she chided herself. The man was only doing his job, and she knew firsthand how good he was at it. Instead of being angry with him for trying to manipulate a confession out of her, she should be glad someone like him had been assigned to the case. She was confident he would soon dig up the truth and find out who had killed Jordan.

Brooke turned up the volume when the camera focused on Mr. Harmon.

"We have suffered a tragedy in our Skytech 1 family," Mr. Harmon said. "This morning, Jordan Lancaster, one of our employees, was found dead in his office on the main floor of the building behind us."

The screen blurred as a new flood of tears filled Brooke's eyes. She dashed them away with the back of her hand.

"Mr. Lancaster joined the company four years ago," Mr. Harmon continued. "He has held several key positions, most recently as manager of the research and development department. He's been a valued member of the management team and a good friend. We feel his loss keenly." He looked directly at the camera. "Our deepest sympathies go out to Mr. Lancaster's wife and daughter."

"How did he die?" someone off camera called out.

Mr. Harmon's jaw tightened, but he spoke in the same calm tone. "We're not ready to release that information yet, but the circumstances of his death are suspicious."

The buzz of voices rose, and more questions were shouted.

"What do you mean by 'suspicious'? Was it an accident?"

"Was he murdered?"

Mr. Harmon held up a hand to quiet the crowd. "I've been asked not to discuss any details at this time, but let me assure you that the Los Angeles Police Department has our full cooperation."

On cue, Detective Travis unfolded his arms and stepped forward. The camera shifted to center him in the picture.

Brooke switched off the TV. He might be good at his job, but she'd heard enough of Travis's voice today.

Since the official announcement had been made, that meant Holly had been given the news that she was now a widow and a single mother to one-year-old Aria. Should Brooke call her? Express her sympathies and make sure Holly knew she had nothing to do with Jordan's death?

But the only number Brooke had, the one on the contact list for the office, was Jordan's cell. Besides, it was too soon to offer her sympathies. No doubt the poor woman was in shock. She didn't need the comfort of a near stranger. Hopefully she had family with her. Jordan had mentioned Aria staying with Holly's mother once or twice while he took her to dinner.

A dull pain throbbed in Brooke's head. She put her fingers to her temples and tried to massage it away, with no success. Had her coworkers watched the press conference? Did they know?

If she had had any friends in the department, she would have called them. It might help to be able to commiserate with someone who knew Jordan and could share her heartbreak over the loss. But there wasn't a single person she felt close enough to call. Office gossip being what it was, the phone lines were probably on fire right now with employees calling one another, running through a whole list of possible circumstances that had led to Jordan's death.

Her name was most likely being tossed around since she'd been seen leaving the building to which no one else had been admitted. Brooke shifted on the sofa cushion, uncomfortable at the thought of being the topic of the office grapevine. Would they suspect her? If Detective Travis had his way, they certainly would.

But that was a temporary situation. By now the police had probably reviewed the security records. There were no cameras inside the administrative offices, but they would check the recordings from the one outside the north entrance. They would inspect the access logs and see that she'd badged into the building at 7:15, and they'd check her office phone records and notice that she'd placed the panicked call to Ed at . . . Well, she didn't know what time, but it couldn't have been that long after she arrived. Certainly not enough time to strangle a man.

Once again the image of Jordan's body rose like a specter in her mind's eye. Brooke felt the crunch of glass beneath her shoe and saw the black cord looped around his neck. A wave of nausea washed through her, settling in the pit of her stomach.

She needed a distraction. Otherwise, that vision would keep circling over and over. What should she do? Watch television? Read a book? She wouldn't be able to concentrate on either. What would help her scrub that image out of her mind?

Brooke jumped off the couch, sending the cat sprawling.

Sammy yowled a protest as he landed abruptly on the floor.

"Sorry." She bent down and scratched behind the cat's ears.

Sammy huffed, then raised his head and strolled away.

Brooke grabbed a bucket, a mop, and some cleaning supplies from the broom closet. She'd clean the house from top to bottom.

As she set to work, she pushed all her terrible thoughts away. Instead, she focused on finding every speck of dirt in the house and eradicating it.

Connor tapped his fingers on the steering wheel and watched Brooke Lester's house through the windshield. He'd seen no movement at all since she slammed the door in his face half an hour ago. The notebook on the seat beside him held a few more scribbles, her address, name, and the details of their brief and unenlightening conversation.

His cell phone rang. He snatched it off the dashboard and checked the screen. It was Fitz.

"Are you getting this?" Fitz asked.

His thoughts blanked. "Getting what?"

An exclamation sounded through the phone. "The press conference at Skytech 1. Tell me you're there."

Connor glanced at Brooke's house, which appeared as deserted as it had for the past thirty minutes. "Not exactly. I'm following another lead. An employee who was in the building this morning with the police. The dead guy was her boss, a guy named Jordan."

"Jordan Lancaster," Fitz said. "The whole city knows that. He was identified in the press conference, which is where a top-notch investigative journalist would be."

Connor winced at the barb. "The city might know the name of the dead guy, but they don't know the name of his employee. I'm in front of her house now. I've got a feeling she has the inside scoop."

"Then pry it out of her," Fitz commanded before he ended the call.

Connor opened a browser on his phone and pulled up the livestream of the press conference in time to see Skytech 1's CEO step aside. A grim-faced man who identified himself as Detective Travis with the LAPD began talking.

Connor grabbed his notebook and pen.

"Early this morning, a Skytech 1 employee arrived at work and discovered the victim's body in his office," Travis said. "That employee contacted a member of the executive team who was also in the building at the time. The emergency was reported at 7:27 a.m., and law enforcement arrived on the scene at 7:35."

Voices erupted.

The loudest question came from the female reporter who seemed to be in charge of the story. "How did Mr. Lancaster die?"

The detective's tight lips pried apart enough to answer. "I'm not at liberty to discuss the details of an open case."

"So there is a case," the female reporter said. "Was he murdered?"

The detective's nostrils flared, and then he seemed to get his anger under control. "I will tell you that he did not die of natural causes."

More questions were called out, but the detective spun away from the camera and headed toward the doors. The line of men and women standing behind him parted to let him through, followed by Harmon and the rest of the group.

Marcella Mullins, the VP of media relations, remained. She held a stack of papers. "This is our official statement," she announced as she began handing them out to the reporters and others gathered nearby. "It's all we're at liberty to say at the moment. As Mr. Harmon stated, our thoughts and prayers are with Mr. Lancaster's family. Please respect their privacy and give them time and space to grieve in peace. Thank you for understanding."

Connor swiped the phone screen, and the livestream disappeared. Fitz was probably right. A top-notch journalist would have stayed for the press conference. But the announcements were carefully worded and orchestrated. He doubted he would have heard anything in person that he hadn't heard remotely. The official statement Marcella was distributing would probably be posted on the company's website soon, if it wasn't there already. And Detective Travis certainly wouldn't have told him anything.

He tapped a beat on the steering wheel, thinking. He could probably find out the victim's address and pay a visit to the wife. Regardless of Marcella's request, that was probably where the television reporters would head next. A grieving widow might very well reveal details that the police wouldn't. But Connor detested that kind of reporting. The media preying on the emotions of hurting people was cruel. If that was what Fitz expected him to do, then he'd rather cover the anniversary sale of the local surf shop.

No, he'd stick with his instincts. He regarded Brooke's house. Those tears he'd seen were evidence of sincere grief, but he'd seen something else in her countenance. Maybe fear? What was she afraid of? She had been inside that building, and she knew what had happened. It wouldn't take long for the other reporters to find out who she was and where she lived, if they hadn't already. He'd give her another ten or fifteen minutes before approaching her again. This time he would ask if she'd seen the press conference and try to get her to at least comment on that. It might be an opening to get her talking.

Connor glanced down at his phone to note the time, but when he raised his head, his plan evaporated. A pair of police cruisers turned onto the street, headed toward him. They stopped in front of Brooke's house. One parked across the driveway, blocking any exit the blue Toyota might have attempted.

Uh-oh. Things were about to get interesting. He jabbed at his cell phone screen to activate the camera and hopped out of the car.

Someone pounded on the front door.

On her knees in the short hallway that led to her bedroom, Brooke glanced up from her task of scrubbing the baseboards. That wasn't a polite rapping of knuckles on the door. It was an impervious demand for entry.

Possibilities flitted through her mind. A coworker wanting to ask what she saw in the building this morning? A reporter? She suppressed a shudder. That man from the newspaper hadn't had any trouble finding her, which meant the others wouldn't either. She had nothing to say to the media. Leave that for Marcella and Mr. Harmon and the people who knew how to handle reporters.

The pounding continued.

"Ms. Lester," came a muffled male voice from outside, "this is the Los Angeles Police Department. Open the door, please."

Brooke sucked in a breath. The scrub brush fell from her numb fingers. What could the police want with her? She'd already told Detective Travis everything she knew about a dozen times.

"C-coming," she stammered as she got to her feet. With a measured pace, she approached the door. She paused to draw in a few deep breaths before unlocking the dead bolt and twisting the knob.

On her small front stoop stood two officers in full uniform, handguns in plain view on their belts. She recognized Officer Lewis, who now bore no hint of the sympathetic smile she'd displayed when she'd placed a jacket around Brooke's trembling shoulders. She must have taken a scowling lesson from Detective Travis.

The second officer watched her through cold, steely eyes. "Brooke Elizabeth Lester?" he asked in a voice void of emotion.

Something about hearing her full name announced in that monotone sent a chill racing down Brooke's spine. "Y-yes?"

"We'll need you to come with us, ma'am," the officer said.

"Come where?" Brooke sent a beseeching glance toward Officer Lewis. "Why?"

"Police headquarters," Lewis answered. "For questioning."

"Questioning?" Brooke scrubbed a hand across her mouth. It smelled of pine-scented cleaner. "But I've already told Detective Travis everything I know. You were there."

Lewis's expression remained impassive. "There's new evidence the detective needs to ask you about."

"New evidence?" Brooke repeated. She pressed her hands to her temples, trying to force her thoughts to focus. "I don't understand."

"Ma'am," the male officer said sharply, "we've been authorized to bring you in for questioning even if you're unwilling." He raised a hand and rested it on his utility belt. A pair of handcuffs dangled beneath his fingers.

Brooke gasped. "Am I being arrested?"

"We haven't received an official arrest warrant yet," Officer Lewis told her. "But you are being brought in for questioning on suspicion of murder."

The world careened around her for a moment, and her knees almost gave out. She shook her head in a vain attempt to order her thoughts. "I need my purse. My keys. And I have to feed my cat." A sob choked off the last word.

As if to add his agreement to the request, Sammy gave a loud meow from behind her.

"We can give you a couple of minutes to feed the cat," Lewis said.

"I'll be right out." Brooke started to shut the door.

But the male officer planted his foot firmly inside the threshold, stopping her.

Brooke scooped up Sammy, holding him tightly in her arms, and went into the kitchen. How long would they keep her at police headquarters? She didn't know any of her neighbors, so there was no one she could call to feed the cat.

After setting Sammy down, Brooke pulled the cat food bag out of the cabinet and filled his bowl. She emptied a pouch of wet food on top of the dry stuff. Sammy would think he'd died and gone to heaven, but she wanted to make sure he had plenty to eat while she was gone. She retrieved the biggest mixing bowl she owned and filled it to the brim with water, which she placed next to his food bowl.

Sammy tackled the food like he'd been starving for a week.

When Brooke returned to the door, the male officer placed a strong hand under her arm and propelled her toward the cruiser parked at the end of her driveway. His grip was firm, as if he thought she might make a break for it. Like he thought she was a criminal. A murderer.

Her breath became ragged, and panic squeezed at her chest. Brooke gulped air in great shuddering gasps when the officer opened the back door and firmly forced her inside. In the moment before she sank behind the cage-like partition, she stared frantically around her street. She noticed a man standing on the sidewalk with a cell phone pointed in her direction. He was vaguely familiar, though her thoughts were too muddled to place him. But the compassion in his expression reached out to her across the distance.

Help me! Brooke sent the silent plea mindlessly in the moment before the police door slammed shut, trapping her inside.

The room where they put Brooke couldn't exactly be called a jail cell, but the sign on the wall beside the door read *Holding Cell 3*. Officer Lewis led her inside and shut the door behind her without a word.

Brooke listened, expecting to hear the thud of a lock sliding into place. Nothing. She couldn't keep herself from trying the doorknob, and she wasn't surprised when it didn't budge. It was an automatic lock.

She surveyed the room and had to suppress a wild desire to laugh. It reminded her of a scene from a cop show. A small metal table sat in the center, and two hard-backed chairs were on either side, facing each other. There wasn't another stick of furniture in the room. A large two-way mirror was on the rear wall, and her reflection gawked at her from within the frame. She was gaunt and pale, and black smears of mascara darkened the skin beneath her eyes. She averted her gaze, not from the image of herself but from whoever was watching her from the other side.

Her head ached. Tension had turned the muscles in her neck into knots, and she tried to loosen them without success. How long would they leave her in here? Brooke glanced at the mirror again and considered sitting on the floor beneath it. That way they could only see the top of her head. But in the next moment she dismissed the idea as childish. This was no time for adolescent obstinacy. She needed to review every moment and every step she'd taken from the time she walked through the door at Skytech 1 until the police arrived.

She selected one of the chairs—the one that put her back to the mirror—and sat down to think.

Checking the time on the wall clock became an obsession. Her patience seeped away with every passing minute. When her back stiffened from sitting on the hard chair after an hour, Brooke got up to pace the circumference of the room. At one point she stopped directly in front of the mirror and snapped, "Isn't there a time limit for how long you can keep an innocent person locked up?"

She received no response, of course. Detective Travis and his cohorts were probably sitting on the other side of that mirror, eating lunch and watching her pace like a caged animal.

Speaking of lunch, she hadn't eaten in—she checked the time yet again—more than seven hours, since her breakfast of a protein bar in the car on the way to the office. And she was thirsty. Once acknowledged, the thirst became almost unbearable. Her mouth was as dry as a desert.

Brooke stopped in front of the window again and shouted, "I want some water!" She planted her hands on her hips and didn't bother to filter the sarcasm from her tone. "Is that allowed, or is this some sort of passive torture technique to let me dehydrate until I confess to something I didn't do?"

Again, nothing.

She returned to her pacing, slamming her feet into the bland floor tiles with such force that she wouldn't have been surprised if they cracked. *So much for not acting childish.*

Finally, the door opened, and Detective Travis stepped through, accompanied by a woman whose face might have been carved out of the same block of granite as his. She carried a leather case and a folding chair, which she set up at the small table and slid into.

Brooke barely gave her a glance, because Detective Travis extended a bottle of water.

"Thought you might like a drink," he commented.

"Thank you." She clipped the words short, seized the bottle, and downed half of it in one long gulp.

"Please have a seat, Ms. Lester." Travis pointed toward the chair across the table from the woman, the one facing the mirror.

Tightening her jaw, she perched on the edge of the seat and clutched the water bottle with both hands.

"This is Detective Layne," Travis said.

The woman nodded.

Brooke ignored her and focused on Travis. "Why am I here? I told you everything I know at the office this morning."

"We've uncovered some details I thought might interest you," he said.

"And you couldn't give me a phone call?" she shot back.

Travis ignored the question. "The coroner's preliminary report indicates the time of death at somewhere between 6:20 and 6:40 this morning."

"There you go." Brooke folded her arms across her chest. "I wasn't at work then."

A frigid smile appeared. "We have your official statement." His dark eyes grew intense. "Now we want the truth."

Brooke exploded. "I've told you the truth! Whatever it is you're fishing for, you won't get it from me." She leaned across the table and held his gaze. "I did not kill Jordan. Why won't you believe me?"

"Do you know how the victim died?" Travis asked in the same cold voice.

Once again, the horrible image swam in her memory. "I think he was strangled. I saw a black cord around his neck."

"Exactly. He was strangled with a computer power cable, to be specific." He studied her face. "Do you know where that cable came from?"

A clammy dampness erupted in her palms. "My computer wouldn't power on this morning. I thought it was broken."

Travis gave Detective Layne a slight nod.

The woman opened the leather case and extracted a tablet. She tapped on the screen a few times, then turned it toward Brooke.

It took Brooke a moment to recognize the scene on the small screen. The image was slightly blurry, as though something had partially obscured the camera lens. She realized that it was the side entrance to Skytech 1 Industries, shown from an angle that must have been in a corner above and to the left of the security door. Nothing moved, and she would have assumed it was a photograph except for a timeline in the bottom left corner, ticking off the seconds. The time read 6:04.

"This is the security recording from this morning," Travis explained.

"Why is it so blurry?" Brooke asked.

"Because someone covered the camera with a piece of plastic wrap," he replied. "The culprit apparently thought that would obscure the image without drawing attention to the attempt."

Brooke would have asked another question, but she noticed a figure approach on the screen. At first she didn't recognize him through the spidery creases in the plastic, but then he looked up, and she saw him clearly. Without a doubt, it was Jordan. He carried a coffee cup in one hand and his badge in the other. He held the badge to the reader, paused for the door to unlock, and opened the door.

Detective Layne paused the recording.

Brooke's throat tightened. These were the last images taken of Jordan. "He came to work early," she commented, noting the time. "He doesn't usually get to the office until almost nine."

"His wife said he had an early meeting this morning," Travis said. "But she didn't know who it was with. Only that he hadn't slept at all, and he appeared to be distracted and worried about something."

Brooke knew that Jordan had been upset because of the failed test and having to give a report to Ed. "All the lights were off when I arrived."

"And you claim that was at 7:15?" he asked.

With a scowl at his choice of words, she said, "It was."

One corner of his mouth twitched upward, and the smirk sent a wave of uneasiness through Brooke.

Layne slid her finger across the tablet's screen, and the recording continued. The time now read 6:18. Jordan had been in the building for almost fifteen minutes.

A blurry figure approached the door. Was this the killer? Brooke leaned forward and squinted, trying to make out facial features. But this person wore a UCLA jacket, zipped up to the chin and with the hood pulled fully over their head, which served to shield their identity. The figure was slight and shorter than Jordan.

"Do you own a UCLA jacket like that one?" Travis asked.

"Me and about twenty thousand other people in this city." Brooke peered at the screen and murmured, "If only we could see his face."

Then she caught sight of something that sent a shock of ice through her veins. The figure carried a quilted purse.

Her gaze flew to her own purse, where she'd set it on the edge of the table. It was identical to the one on the security recording.

"But that wasn't me!" Brooke cried out in despair. "Surely you can't think that was me."

Travis remained silent as Layne paused the recording.

"That wasn't me," Brooke repeated. She couldn't believe this was happening. "I couldn't kill anyone. And I didn't kill Jordan. There's no way I could have overpowered a man who works out every day. It's obvious that someone is trying to frame me."

"Evidence doesn't lie," Travis responded, "but killers do."

Layne resumed the recording. The figure on the screen held a badge against the reader and disappeared into the building.

"Check with security," Brooke said. Her voice echoed off the walls of the small room, shrill with panic. She took a breath and spoke more slowly. "They can tell you whose badge opened the door."

Travis nodded at Detective Layne again.

The woman pulled a sheet of paper from her case and slid it across the table toward Brooke. There were two columns of numbers, one labeled *Badge Number* and the second *Time Stamp*. The header identified the report as *Badge Access—North Entrance*. The time stamp on the first row read *06:04:57*, followed by a badge number. The second row read *06:18:23*, followed by a different badge number.

"May I see your badge?" Travis asked Brooke. His voice was now extraordinarily polite, but the eyes that bored into hers were as sharp as flint.

Brooke couldn't muster a word. She struggled to comprehend the data on the report in front of her. She pulled her purse toward her, extracted her badge, and handed it to Travis as hopelessness sank into her spine.

It was her badge number shown entering the building at 6:18 this morning. Just minutes before Jordan was strangled to death.

Connor shifted his weight on the hard bench in the front waiting room of LAPD headquarters. He'd been sitting in this same spot for three hours. His article, which held frustratingly little information beyond the basics that had already been reported by every television station in the city, had been written on his laptop and sent to Fitz two hours ago. A parade of people came and went through the lobby, but there was still no sign of Brooke.

He approached the reception counter. Smiling broadly at the woman behind the bulletproof glass panel, he opened his mouth to ask a question.

"No, she hasn't left yet," the brunette told him with an exasperated sigh. "And no, I haven't been told that she's being taken to a cell." She raised an eyebrow. "Yet."

"Just checking." Connor awarded her a wide smile, which she did not return.

He paced back to his bench. What was he doing here anyway? He should be planted outside Skytech 1 Industries, ready to pounce on anyone who left the building. Preferably not Marcella Mullins, who'd been trained to handle the press, but an unwary executive who might let something new slip.

Still, Connor couldn't shake the memory of Brooke being taken away in a police car. That desperate look she'd given him. His mother always said he'd been born with a heart for the underdog, and it had gotten him into trouble more than once.

He took his cell phone out of his pocket and scrolled through the pictures he'd snapped of Brooke. The one as she sped past his car on the way out of the parking lot had caught her in the middle of a sob. Then the last one, her expression full of despair. His chest tightened as he studied the snapshot. How could he ignore her silent plea for help?

A buzz sounded, and the security door opened. Brooke stepped through, her arms wrapped around her purse, clutching it to her chest. She walked a few steps into the room and then stopped and cast a dazed glance around.

Connor jumped off the bench and approached her. "Remember me?"

"Yeah. You're . . ." She scrubbed at her forehead, as though trying to dislodge a name.

"Connor Dyson."

"That's right. The newspaper reporter who found my license plate number and stopped by my house." She brushed past him, heading for the exit.

Snatching his laptop from the bench, he dashed after her in time to lurch ahead and open the door.

Brooke narrowed her eyes, then left the building and stepped into the sunshine. Squinting, she unzipped her purse and shoved one hand inside. "Oh no," she muttered. "My sunglasses are in my car."

"I have an extra pair in my glove compartment," Connor offered.

"What are you doing here?" she demanded. "Do you make a habit of hanging out at the police station, hoping to get a juicy lead or something?"

Heat rose up his neck. "Actually, I was waiting for you. I thought you might need a ride home."

"Yeah?" Brooke asked, pinning him with a glare. "In return for what?"

"Hey." Connor held up his hands as if to ward off her scowl. "I'm just trying to be helpful."

She remained silent as she studied him.

Clearly she didn't believe him, and he couldn't blame her.

"Okay, I was hoping you'd tell me what happened this morning," Connor admitted. "But the offer of a ride is real."

"No thanks." Brooke spun away, scanning the distance.

In profile with her head held high, she was almost regal. It was strange for someone who'd spent hours in police custody. Not many people would be able to keep their emotions in check after the shock of losing their boss under suspicious circumstances and then being hauled in for questioning. He couldn't help but admire her composure.

"You don't have a car," he pointed out.

"I'm sure there's a taxi nearby."

"But I'm free," Connor said, adding a tempting tone to his voice. She stared at him.

He winced. Did she think he was flirting with her? "What I mean is, I won't charge you. Do you know how much taxis cost these days? The price of gas and all that. Not that I'd charge you for gas," he rushed to clarify, then shut his mouth. He sounded like a babbling teenager. Maybe he *was* flirting.

"Well," Brooke said slowly, "I do need a ride."

"Great. I'm parked over here." Connor led her to his car, opened the passenger door for her, and pointed to the glove compartment. "The sunglasses are in there." He closed the door and rounded the front bumper. When he slid behind the wheel, he saw that she had found the glasses and also his stash.

"Gummy worms?" She held the package toward him, one eyebrow raised in a question.

"Yeah." He gave a rueful chuckle as he started the engine. "I've loved them since I was a kid. Help yourself."

"One worm probably has more sugar than I usually eat in a week." Brooke opened the bag and fished out a long red piece of candy. "But I am really hungry."

"You want to stop for a burger or something?" He winced again. What was he doing? This wasn't a date.

"Thanks, but I just want to go home," she said, yawning. "It's been a long day."

Connor glanced at her as he headed for the highway. His oversize sunglasses all but hid her slender face.

Brooke tore the candy in half and chewed with relish. "It might be pure sugar, but it tastes great right now." She leaned her head back against the headrest and ate the other half.

He merged into traffic. "Do you mind telling me what you were doing at the police department for so long?"

"Yes, I do." A long silence followed. Then she asked, "Can this be an off-the-record conversation?"

It wasn't exactly what he wanted, but at the moment he felt like she needed a friendly ear, not a journalist. "Sure."

"The police think I killed my boss."

"Why would they think that?" Connor asked. He couldn't imagine why this woman sitting beside him would be a murder suspect.

Brooke gave a heavy sigh. "There's some sort of mix-up with the security system. They say my employee badge was recorded going into the building shortly before . . ." She swallowed visibly. "Before Jordan died. But that's a mistake or else—"

What had she been about to say? "Do mistakes like that happen often with the security system?"

"Never. At least not that I know of." Fishing out another gummy worm from the bag, she shook her head. "I can't explain it. And there were a couple of other weird things. Incriminating things."

"Such as?" Connor prompted.

"I'd rather not say." Brooke ripped off the sunglasses and glared at him. "But I didn't kill Jordan. I wouldn't. It's unthinkable."

Her words rang with sincerity. Perhaps it was a journalist's instinct, but he believed her. "How did he die?"

"He was strangled with a computer power cable." She examined a green worm. "It was mine."

Connor let the news settle, his mind racing. A mix-up with her badge. Her computer cable used as the murder weapon. Maybe he was off base, but she struck him as an intelligent woman, too intelligent to leave so much evidence behind.

"It sounds like somebody's trying pretty hard to make it look like you killed him," he said.

Brooke shifted in her seat. "That's what I said. I told Detective Travis somebody is trying to frame me. It's couldn't be more obvious."

He remembered the detective from this morning's press conference. "What did he say?"

Her shoulders slumped. "He said evidence doesn't lie, but killers do."

Connor took the next exit, his mind whirling. "I don't think he really suspects you," he told her when he'd settled into a line of traffic. "Otherwise, he wouldn't have let you go. He would have charged you with murder and locked you up."

"I hope you're right," she responded. "He mentioned something about waiting for physical evidence from the lab, fingerprints or something. But I'm not supposed to go anywhere."

"You didn't ask for my advice, but here's what I think you should do," Connor said. "You need to make a public statement saying you're innocent. Describe exactly what happened and convince people that you're not a killer. And do it before the police charge you with anything. Public opinion is a pretty powerful force."

"To whom would I make such a statement?" Brooke asked, suspicion creeping into her voice.

He couldn't meet her gaze. "Well, me for a start."

"I knew it," she snapped. "You're just being nice to me because you want a story. You'll write an article about the accused murderer and get a raise or win a Pulitzer or whatever it is you're after."

"That is not true," Connor said evenly. "I said you should start with me. Once people read my article in tomorrow's paper, you'll have TV news crews camped outside your house. Talk to them. Put yourself in the public eye, and convince them you're innocent before the police have a chance to tell them otherwise."

Brooke pointedly ignored him. She stared out the window as he spoke, strands of dark hair waving gently in the car's air-conditioning.

He navigated through the side streets of her neighborhood, itching to ask what she was thinking yet somehow certain he shouldn't.

When Connor pulled up in front of her house, he parked and waited, unsure of what to do or say.

Brooke turned to him, her eyes blazing with fury. "You are despicable." She spat the word. "First you run my license plate to find out where I live. Then you come to my house to try to pry a story out of me. And when that didn't work, you loiter in the lobby of the police department, waiting for me to come out so you could pretend to be my friend. All because you want to be the first one with the breaking news." She waved a hand in the air, as though reciting a headline. "'My Interview with Murderer Brooke Lester.'"

"No, that's not true," he said.

She shoved the car door open, hopped out, and rushed to the front door.

Connor followed her. "Listen to me. You're upset. I get that." He tried to keep his tone soothing.

Brooke fumbled with her keys. "Oh really?" A humorless laugh blasted from her lips. "Listen, buster, you haven't seen upset yet." She raised a finger and jabbed it at his chest. "Our off-the-record talk had better stay that way. If you write one word about me in that paper of yours, I'll sue you for everything you've got."

Anger flared in his gut, and he resisted the urge to rub his chest where she'd probably left a small bruise. With an enormous effort, he clenched his jaw to stop a heated reply. Maybe she wasn't holding up as well after the stress of the day as he'd thought.

"I always keep my word," Connor told her through gritted teeth.

That seemed to deflate her a little. She remained silent, but a bit of the suspicion still seeped from her.

He removed his wallet from his hip pocket, extracted a business card, and dropped it into her open purse. "Call me if you change your mind about talking and want someone in the media on your side."

"Yeah, right." And for the second time that day, Brooke Lester slammed her door in his face.

As usual, the alarm beeped at six o'clock. Brooke pried her eyes open. She'd finally fallen asleep around four. From the kitchen she heard the sound of the automatic coffee maker dripping and caught the first bracing whiff of her usual morning pick-me-up. But with five hours' sleep in two days, no amount of caffeine could make her feel alert.

Beside her, Sammy stretched and gave voice to a chirping purr, his way of greeting the day. He rolled toward her and nestled against her side, soft and warm.

She soaked up the cat's comforting presence and snuggled deeper into the covers. Maybe she should call in sick. Stay in bed all day, and get some more sleep. Mr. Harmon had advised her to take a few days off, and no one would blame her.

But whom could she call? Ed, who already thought she was a weak female?

And what of Detective Travis? If Brooke altered her regular routine, would he somehow use that as evidence of her guilt? Even as the thought occurred to her, she realized its source was a growing paranoia caused by Travis's ridiculous accusations. Still, maintaining a sense of normalcy in high-stress situations was probably the best course of action.

On the other hand, nothing could induce her to be the first person in the building this morning. The idea of entering the dark office left her cold. She should sleep for a couple more hours.

But her mind was already churning with the events of yesterday. No way would she be able to sleep now. Heaving a resigned sigh, she threw the covers back and slipped out of bed.

Brooke pulled into the nearly full parking lot at nine o'clock. Satisfied that the workday was already underway, she approached the side entrance. She pressed her badge against the electronic reader.

Nothing.

With a sinking feeling, she tried again, but the red light indicating the door was locked didn't blink.

It wasn't a big surprise that she'd been locked out. After all, if someone had forged her badge, then the security department would have had to deactivate it. It made sense.

Brooke followed the sidewalk around the building and entered through the visitor entrance. Inside, she greeted the receptionist and was satisfied when the woman gave her a pleasant smile. At least she hadn't been banned from the office. That was a good sign.

The somber mood in the R & D department crushed any comfort she might have taken from the receptionist's smile. The place was normally full of different sounds—the tapping of keyboards, Larry's music playing quietly from his cubicle, and the hum of voices. But today a heavy silence permeated the room. She passed Greg's cubicle on her way to her desk. He sat unmoving in his chair, his computer monitor dark, staring with an unfocused gaze toward Jordan's office.

Derek popped up from his chair and followed her into her cubicle. He jerked his head toward the dark office. "All Jordan's stuff is gone."

"The police cleaned out his office yesterday." Brooke opened the bottom desk drawer to drop her purse and lunch bag inside. "Searching for clues, I guess."

Larry joined them and fixed a troubled gaze on her. "Was it, you know, awful? Finding him, I mean."

Her stomach tightened as she fought against the image that tried to force its way into her mind. "Yeah, it was awful."

"I can't believe he's dead." Derek shook his head. "Everybody liked Jordan. Who would want to kill him? And why?"

Apparently they hadn't heard that she was considered a suspect. What would they think if she were arrested for Jordan's murder? With evidence like the security records, it was a real possibility. Detective Travis might show up here any minute and take her into custody.

Brooke pushed the thought from her mind. If she focused on what might happen, she'd go crazy. In all likelihood Travis had already figured out that she was being framed and was searching for the real killer. Connor Dyson had said the same thing yesterday. The police wouldn't have released her if they thought she was a murderer. Right?

Out of habit she pushed the button on her computer to turn it on. When nothing happened, a weird déjà vu struck her, and again she had to force yesterday's visions from her mind. Her power cord was probably in a police evidence locker somewhere. It was a murder weapon now.

"I've got to run over to tech support," she told the guys. "I'll be back in a few minutes."

Brushing past them, Brooke left the department. Before she picked up a power cable, she decided to stop by the security office for a new badge. She walked through the hallways, nodding at the people she passed. The bleak atmosphere was not confined to the R & D department. Naturally everyone had heard of the tragedy, and she encountered very few smiles. Some avoided her gaze completely, and one woman even sped up to pass her, head down.

They know I found him, she consoled herself. *They're uncomfortable. Not suspicious.*

But when Brooke arrived at the security office, there could be little doubt that news of the police's suspicions had reached her coworkers.

Rick, the man seated in front of a dozen computer monitors, greeted her with unmasked hostility. "What are you doing here?" he demanded.

"I came to get a new badge." She extended hers. "Mine doesn't work."

"Of course not," he snapped. "I deactivated it yesterday when I pulled the access report for the police."

Brooke stiffened. "That was not my badge. It couldn't have been. I didn't get here yesterday until seven fifteen."

"It was your badge all right." Thick wire-rimmed glasses magnified the glare Rick aimed at her. "I'm surprised the police are letting you run around free. How could you do something like that? Jordan was a nice guy, a family man. You are one sick woman."

Dumbfounded, she took a step forward.

He rolled his chair backward and raised his hands, eyes behind the thick lenses suddenly round as cantaloupes. "Don't come near me. I know karate."

A wild laugh gathered in her chest, but Brooke stifled it. This wasn't funny. "Come on. You can't really believe I could kill anyone. Jordan worked out every day. There's no way I could have overpowered him." She'd voiced the same argument many times to Detective Travis, but he'd refused to listen.

At least Rick seemed open to considering her words. He cocked his head and squinted at her thin frame. "You don't look very strong."

"You know this security system better than anyone," she said, changing the subject. "You're the expert."

His chest inflated. "I know it inside out."

"Then you know it can be hacked."

Rick drew a breath to voice an argument.

Brooke rushed on before he could say anything. "That's the only feasible explanation. Somebody made a duplicate badge and used it yesterday morning."

"Impossible." He shook his head. "The system keeps records of every badge created. I searched the database, and there has been exactly one badge issued with your number. That was the day you were hired."

"Databases can be altered," she countered. "Records can be erased."

Rick continued to shake his head. "That would take someone with a lot of skill and an in-depth knowledge of the security system."

"We work for a technology company," Brooke pointed out. "There are at least twenty-five people in this building who could hack that system if they wanted to."

"Including you," he said.

She sighed. This conversation was getting her nowhere. "I guess we'll have to let the police figure it out. Can I have a new badge, please?"

"Nope." Rick twirled his chair toward the bank of monitors.

"Why not?"

"Not my call," he said without turning. "Talk to Ed Gentry. He's the one who told me to lock you out."

Brooke should have known that the director who had barely spoken five sentences to her in six months was responsible. Resentment rose inside her and with it a rush of anger. Why would Ed lock her out of the building without telling her? Didn't she deserve the common courtesy of an explanation?

"I'll be back," she told Rick. Then she marched out of the security office.

Bypassing the elevator, she stomped up the stairs to the second floor and entered the hallway everyone referred to as Directors' Row.

Ed's assistant, stationed at her desk outside his office, gaped as Brooke breezed past, opened the door, and barged into the room.

"Why have I been locked out of the building?" she demanded.

Seated behind an immaculate desk, the director watched her calmly, as if he had irate women storm into his office every ten minutes. "I would think the reason is obvious," Ed said.

"It was not my badge yesterday morning." Her chest heaved with fury. "Someone is trying very hard to frame me, but I did not kill Jordan."

"I'm sure the police are taking every possibility into account in their investigation," Ed said. "No doubt this whole thing will be resolved soon."

His ingratiating smile rubbed like sandpaper on her raw nerves. Her nails bit into the palms of her hands as she clenched her fists.

"In the meantime, I think it would be a good idea for you to take a leave of absence," he continued.

The anger dissolved, leaving her limp. "A leave of absence?"

"With pay, of course." The director's smile deepened. "Just until you're cleared. I'm sure you understand."

Brooke certainly understood. The company wanted her gone so if charges were officially filed against her, they could claim that they'd already taken steps to remove her. They probably had a statement drawn up and ready to deliver to the press.

"Now, if you'll excuse me, I've got a busy day ahead of me." Ed gestured toward the door.

Numb, Brooke left his office and returned to her desk. She ignored the stares from her coworkers as she gathered her purse and lunch bag.

She vowed to clear her name. No matter how long it took.

Connor sat in a chair in the small reception area outside Skytech 1's media relations department.

Marcella's office door was closed. Though the man stationed at the desk in front of it assured Connor that she would see him after she finished her conference call, he was beginning to suspect they were toying with him. That call had already lasted forty-five minutes. Twenty minutes ago, the sound of a female's muffled voice went silent. Was there a separate exit in the office? Maybe Marcella had slipped out to avoid meeting with him. Or maybe she was trying to wait him out. Well, he had a list of questions and a whole day to spend on getting answers.

Connor shifted in the chair and propped an ankle on the opposite knee, gazing through the windows at the view of the parking lot. The palm fronds on the trees lining the lot swayed in a warm September breeze. A woman rounded the corner of the building, and he idly watched her weave through the parked cars, clutching a purse to her chest with both arms. She seemed familiar.

He leaped out of his chair.

The guy at the desk looked questioningly at him.

"I just remembered another appointment," Connor said as he dashed out of the office.

The media relations department was located in the front of the building, not far from the main entrance. Connor jogged through the hallway and out the door, disregarding the curious glances cast his way.

Outside, he broke into a run and managed to intercept Brooke as she reached her blue Toyota. "Hey," he said, chest heaving with his effort. "I thought that was you."

She appeared troubled, but when she recognized him, her worry seemed to melt into irritation. "You again? Do I need to file a restraining order against you?" She set her purse on the hood of the car and rummaged inside.

"I'm not following you," Connor insisted.

Brooke paused her search long enough to raise her eyebrows skeptically at him.

He held up his hands, palms splayed. "Honest. I was trying to get in to see Ms. Mullins to get an official statement when I saw you leave the building."

"Maybe you should go back inside," she suggested. "You'll have more success getting her to talk than me."

"Actually, I was getting ready to leave anyway. I think she's avoiding me."

Brooke snorted. "Imagine that." She extracted a set of car keys from her purse and pressed a button on the fob. The Toyota's lock clicked open.

Connor took a sideways step that put him between her and the driver's side door. "Listen, we got off on the wrong foot when I ran your plates. I understand why you'd feel like that was a breach of privacy. Please accept my apology."

She nodded slightly. "Apology accepted."

"Thank you." He leaned his hip against the car door. "I know you think I'm only after a story, but I really can help you. I'm a journalist. I'm good at digging up facts."

At least she didn't dismiss him out of hand. Instead, she tilted her head and appraised him for a long moment.

Connor returned her gaze, trying his best to show her that he was sincere.

"Why do you want to help me?" Brooke asked. "I mean, other

than the fact that you want an exclusive interview with a suspected murderer." She winced when she spoke the last word.

A list of reasons filtered through his head. Because he was a good writer whose skills were being wasted reporting cases of food poisoning at the local snack shop. Because he needed a sensational story to get the attention of the senior editors at the newspaper. Because if he did decide to leave LA, he wanted to go out with a bang instead of slinking back to Ohio with his tail between his legs.

Because Brooke Lester appeared vulnerable and defenseless, and he wanted to help her. But he dared not voice the thought, hardly dared to admit it to himself.

"I want the truth," Connor finally answered. "Same as you. And I think if we work together, we can find it faster than either of us could alone."

Brooke regarded him as though weighing whether he was feeding her a line or telling the truth.

Her cell phone rang. She dug it out of her purse. As she glanced at the screen, the color drained from her face.

"Is it the police?" he asked.

Brooke shook her head and pressed a button. "Hello?" She paused and squeezed her eyes shut. "I'm so sorry." Another pause. "Yes, of course I will. What's the address?" She reached into her purse and extracted a wrinkled piece of paper, which she smoothed out on the Toyota's hood.

Connor whipped a pen out from his notebook and handed it to her.

She flashed him an unreadable expression, then scribbled on the paper. "I'll be right there," she said into the phone and disconnected the call.

"Where are we going?" he asked.

Brooke pursed her lips, then appeared to reach a decision. "We're going to Jordan's house." She handed him the pen. "To talk to his wife."

The Lancasters lived in Calabasas, about thirty miles from Los Angeles. Brooke's GPS estimated the trip would take half an hour. She kept her focus on the road as she drove, though she was acutely aware of Connor in the Toyota's passenger seat, scribbling in his notebook.

Had she made a mistake, inviting him to come along? He was a journalist and good at digging up facts, as she knew from personal experience. She was great at combing through computer code, but she wasn't as comfortable talking to people. When Holly called, Brooke had still been reeling from the disturbing conversation with Ed, and Connor's offer of assistance had felt very much like a life preserver tossed to a drowning woman.

"You're not planning to interview Holly Lancaster, are you?" Brooke watched him out of the corner of her eye. "I mean, she just lost her husband in a terrible way, and I don't want you to upset her by asking a bunch of questions."

Connor gave her an injured look. "Give me a little credit, would you? I'm not heartless, you know."

"No, I don't." She tightened her grip on the wheel. "From the little I know of you, you're ambitious and pushy, and reporters aren't typically known for their sensitivity."

"Journalists," he corrected.

Brooke shrugged. "Same difference."

"They're not the same. Technically, a reporter is a type of journalist, but the general consensus is that the word *reporter* refers to a broadcast journalist. I'm an investigative journalist, a writer."

"Thanks for the lesson in journalistic terminology," she told him drily. "But while we're there, try to keep your investigative tendencies under control." She sobered. "Holly is nice, and I don't want to add to her pain."

Connor answered with a nod and returned to scribbling in his notebook.

Curious, she asked, "If you're not making notes about questions to ask, what are you doing?"

"Writing a letter to my mother," he replied. "She prefers them to e-mails. Says seeing my handwriting and holding the same paper I've held makes her feel closer to me."

How sweet. Somehow Brooke hadn't thought about this guy having a mother and a soft side that wanted to please her. She spared a quick glance down at the notebook. Rows of neat, even handwriting already filled half the page.

By the time she pulled into the Calabasas neighborhood, he'd finished his letter and closed his notebook. Brooke followed the disembodied voice from the GPS through the streets and arrived at an attractive ranch-style home. A stone walkway carved the manicured lawn in half and led from the sidewalk to a front porch lined with columns. Three cars filled the wide driveway, so Brooke parked on the street in front of the house.

She rounded the front of the car and joined Connor on the sidewalk. "I'm going to introduce you as a friend, okay? Not a journalist. Because this is an off-the-record talk, right?"

He held up three fingers. "Scout's honor. At least until we have the full story."

"Agreed."

They approached the house, but before Brooke could knock, the front door opened.

Holly stood inside, her face haggard with grief. When she saw Brooke, her eyes filled with tears, and she held out her arms.

Though they barely knew each other, Brooke didn't hesitate to step into the embrace. Shared grief formed a bond that hadn't existed before, and for a long moment they indulged in communal tears.

Holly pulled away first, wiping her cheeks with the back of her hand. "Just when I think I've cried myself dry, here come the waterworks again."

"I understand." Brooke brushed at her cheeks. "I can't believe he's gone."

"I know." Holly swallowed hard, then held out a hand to Connor. "Hello."

"Connor Dyson." He shook her hand. "I'm sorry for your loss."

"Connor is a friend. He was with me when you called." A touch of heat erupted in Brooke's cheeks. Would Holly think the guy was her boyfriend?

"Please come inside." Holly stepped back to allow them to enter the house.

Brooke found herself in a living room that could have been featured in an interior design magazine. Wide and expansive, the elegant room stretched all the way to the rear of the house. White sofas with accent pillows formed a conversation nook around a coffee table with a smoked glass surface. The back wall consisted of floor-to-ceiling windows that offered a view of a huge patio and an in-ground pool. Lush greenery surrounded the pool, dotted here and there with colorful flowers, and a waterfall flowed from a spa at the far end. Three women sat poolside, and a fourth waded waist-deep through the water holding little Aria, who kicked and splashed.

"My mom and sisters," Holly explained. "Jordan's parents are flying in tonight to help plan the . . . funeral."

Brooke battled the prickle of tears. Jordan's funeral. It still didn't seem real. Except she knew it was real. She had seen his body herself. She suppressed a shudder.

"I'd like to speak privately with Brooke for a minute," Holly said to Connor. "Would you mind having a seat here?"

Brooke thought he might balk, but he didn't hesitate even for an instant.

"Of course." Connor gestured toward the pool area. "If you don't mind, I'll go introduce myself."

"Please do," Holly said.

Brooke followed Holly from the room. A backward glance showed Connor opening the French doors and stepping out onto the patio. Brooke and Holly made their way down a short hallway and into an office, where Holly closed the door.

"Ed came by last night," Holly said, approaching a desk.

Brooke wondered why Holly was telling her this.

"He brought Jordan's car, and his gym bag was in it." Holly picked up a canvas bag from the floor and set it on the surface of the desk. "I couldn't even open it last night. It was too much."

Sympathy stabbed at Brooke. "I understand."

Holly flashed a grateful smile. "This morning I went through it. I wanted to hold something that smelled like him, you know? Even if it was his sweaty gym clothes." A humorless laugh fell flat between them. "But that's not what I found."

Brooke moved closer.

Holly pulled out a stack of neatly folded clothing. "They haven't been worn. They still smell like fabric softener."

Brooke shook her head. "I don't understand."

"Jordan left the house really early yesterday to go to the gym." Holly set the clothes on the desk. "But he didn't work out."

Brooke still didn't understand. She waited for Holly to explain.

"And then there's this." Holly removed two items from the bag and handed them both to her.

Brooke studied them. One was a sales receipt from a store in Calabasas, dated the day before at 05:12:08 a.m. The other was a small card with three numbers printed on it.

Holly tapped the receipt. "That store is located between here and the gym we're members of. See what he bought?"

The receipt showed two items. A cup of coffee from the deli department and a heavy-duty combination lock. Brooke held up the card. "This must be the combination to the lock he purchased."

Holly nodded.

"So what exactly happened?" Brooke asked, trying to wrap her mind around the situation.

"He worked all night Wednesday night," Holly told her. "He was very uptight about something. He woke me up a little before five to kiss me goodbye. He said he had an emergency meeting, and he needed to go to the gym first to work off some stress."

"Was the meeting with Ed?"

Holly shrugged. "He didn't say."

Brooke frowned at the sales receipt. A combination lock. And the store was near the gym, where Jordan had said he was going but hadn't exercised. She extended the receipt and the card toward Holly. "You should give these to the police."

Holly didn't accept them. Instead, she put her hands behind her back. "I probably should. But somehow I don't think Jordan would want that. There was some big project going on at work, something he was involved in."

"I'm working on the new storage array too," Brooke remarked. "We all are."

"It wasn't like Jordan to get so invested in a work project, but this one was important to him. It was personal, like he felt a sense of ownership or something."

"It's his brainchild," Brooke said. "He's been working on it for years. And it's a big deal. It could revolutionize the data storage industry and catapult Skytech 1 to the top of the field."

"That's what he said. But in the past few days he's been really worried about something. He didn't say what, and I probably wouldn't have understood if he had tried to explain. And then Wednesday when he got home from work, he was frantic. I've never seen him so upset. Something about a test?"

"We were all pretty upset about it. It should have been routine, one of the final steps before we move into the next phase." Brooke sighed. "None of us expected it to fail."

"But that's the thing," Holly said. "Jordan did. Wednesday night he was beating himself up. He kept saying, 'I should have done something, but I kept hoping I was wrong.'"

Until this moment, Brooke had assumed whoever killed Jordan had some personal motive. Or maybe they'd been in the building for another purpose, like theft, and Jordan had happened to be at work early that morning. But based on what Holly was saying, Jordan's murder might be directly linked to the company's ten-drive stripe storage array.

"That's even more reason you should go to the police." Brooke set the receipt and the card down on the desk.

"You know what will happen to that project if the police think it has anything to do with Jordan's death," Holly said. "They'll put a stop to it. They'll call in experts to go over all the technical stuff, and it will take months. From what Jordan told me, that could cause serious problems for the company. It might even go bankrupt."

What she said was true. Ed's comment at the department meeting echoed in Brooke's head. Skytech 1 had sunk millions of dollars into this new technology. *We will have a ten-drive stripe storage array ready to show the shareholders by September 30, or there won't be a single person in this room who still has a job on October 1.*

"Ed will know what to do with the card and the receipt," Brooke said.

Holly shook her head. "Jordan didn't think much of Ed professionally. Or personally, to be honest. He always said Ed's ambitions get in the way of his humanity."

An apt description of the demanding director if Brooke ever heard one.

"But Jordan thought so much of you." Holly held her gaze. "He told me more than once that you were the most intelligent person he'd ever met. That's why I called you."

"What can I do?" Brooke asked.

"When you find whatever he locked up with that combination lock, you'll know what, if it has anything to do with this project," Holly replied. "Then if you think we should hand it over to the police, we will. But if you can figure out who killed him and hand the murderer over to the police at the same time, then maybe Jordan's project won't suffer."

Brooke wanted to say no. A voice in her head shouted, *Mistake!* But she couldn't turn away from Holly's grief. Jordan's widow was asking her for a favor. How could she refuse?

She picked up the receipt and the card with the combination. "What's the name of the gym?"

Connor stared at the receipt in his left hand and three numbers that must be a combination in his right. He studied Brooke in the driver's seat and couldn't help admiring her profile. Artists would itch to paint a profile that beautiful, even with worry lines creasing the otherwise smooth skin of a classic high forehead.

"You're making an assumption the lock is at the gym," he told her.

"Where else could it be? We don't have lockers at the office. I'm not aware of anywhere else that has them other than amusement parks, and they aren't open at five thirty in the morning."

Connor could name a few other places, like the train station or the airport. But neither of those were nearby, so he didn't bother to mention them. Jordan's gym was always open, making it the most logical place for him to store something that could be padlocked.

"What are we going to do with whatever it is when we get it?" he asked.

The GPS announced an upcoming right turn. Brooke put on her blinker and changed lanes before answering. "That depends on what it is. If it doesn't have anything to do with the storage array project, I'll take it straight to Detective Travis."

Connor noticed a slight tremor in her voice when she mentioned the detective. "And if it's somehow related to Skytech 1?"

The creases on her brow deepened. "Then I guess I'll do what Holly suggested—take it home and see if I can figure out what Jordan found that worried him so much."

"Not only worried him," he said in a quiet voice. "Whatever is in that locker might be the reason he was killed."

Brooke glanced at him. "I know."

A battle formed in Connor's mind. He was thoroughly invested in this story. It was much more interesting than any news he'd ever investigated. Thus far, the biggest news break of his career was when a dry cleaner was robbed by a street gang led by the owner's grandson. But this story had the possibility of slinging Connor several notches up the ladder. Maybe even getting him permanently assigned to the news desk.

On the other hand, a man had been murdered. What if finding whatever Jordan Lancaster stashed in that locker put Brooke in danger of becoming the next victim?

"For the record, I think you should give it to Travis without examining it yourself," Connor said. "In fact, I'm going on record by saying we should go to the police right now and hand these over to him." He held up the receipt and the card.

Brooke didn't respond right away. She remained fully focused on steering into the parking lot of the gym and navigating into a parking space. When she'd shut the engine off and unsnapped her seat belt, she plucked the receipt and the card out of his hand. "Thanks for the advice. But I made a promise to my boss's widow, and I intend to keep it."

Connor looked at her. Determination sparked on her features, and he'd rarely seen a jaw so stubbornly set. Worry still niggled in the back of his mind, but if she were resolute—and he had no doubt of that—then he was going to stick to her like flypaper. For the story, yes, but more importantly because he wanted to be on hand to help if she got into trouble.

"All right," he said. "Let's do this."

"You don't have to be involved," she said. "Actually I'm not sure I want you involved."

"Ah, but you need me. You think those gym rats are going to let you waltz into the men's locker room?" Connor held out his hand for the card and watched her struggle with the decision.

Finally, she set the card with the combination in his palm. "So what do we say when we go inside?"

"We can pose as a couple who just moved into the area and are searching for a gym," he suggested.

"How about brother and sister?"

"How many siblings go to the gym together?"

"True." Brooke opened the car door. "Let's get this over with."

Connor couldn't help a tiny smirk as they exited the car.

Connor jumped ahead to open the front door at the gym for Brooke.

Aware that the muscle-bound man behind the counter was watching, she awarded Connor a broad smile as she walked inside. "Thank you," she told him.

"You're welcome, honeybunch," he replied with an even bigger smile.

With an effort, Brooke stifled a sigh. She'd agreed to pose as a couple searching for a new gym. But *honeybunch*? She cocked one eyebrow at him, then smiled at the man behind the counter. "Hello."

The man returned Brooke's smile but simply nodded at Connor. "I'm Chaz."

"Brooke and Connor," she said.

"What can I do for you?" Chaz asked.

"We're new to the area, and we were driving by and thought we'd stop in to see what kind of equipment you have." Brooke made a show of glancing around the large room, which was filled with various types of exercise machines. Along the rear wall stood a bank of lockers, but they were too far away to see if any of them were closed with a shiny new lock.

"As you can see, we offer state-of-the-art equipment." Chaz inflated his burly chest. "And we keep everything in tip-top shape."

"Mind if we explore a bit?" Connor asked.

"Let me give you a tour," Chaz said as he started to rise.

"Oh, that's not necessary," Brooke assured him quickly. "We can wander around ourselves."

"Sorry, but that's against our rules." Chaz rounded the counter and joined them. "No nonmembers in the facility without a staff person. It's a safety thing."

Brooke and Connor exchanged glances. They had to come up with a way to ditch this guy. Or at least distract him.

"Okay, lead on," she said brightly.

Chaz walked them past two rows of treadmills, followed by a row of ellipticals and stationary bicycles. About half of the equipment was in use, the occupants glued to the television screens suspended from the ceiling in front of them.

"Over here are the resistance machines." Chaz pointed out a cluster of various exercise apparatuses, then guided them to an area in the back corner with a huge selection of free weights and weight benches.

Brooke caught Connor's eye and nodded toward the lockers lining the opposite corner.

"What's over there?" Connor asked, motioning toward the lockers.

"We hold aerobics classes there," Chaz said.

"Now we're talking my kind of exercise." Brooke headed in that direction.

"We have some really good instructors," Chaz said as he followed her. "We offer all kinds of classes." He came up beside her and cast an admiring glance down her frame. "You seem like you're into yoga."

Though nothing could have been further from the truth, Brooke smiled at him. "How did you guess?"

"You're fit and toned." Chaz lowered his voice and added a hint of gravel. "And you move with so much grace."

She couldn't believe Chaz was flirting with her when her supposed boyfriend was standing right next to them. This guy had nerve, but maybe she could work this to her favor. "Thank you," she said in a soft voice as she batted her eyelashes a couple of times.

Behind him, Connor put a hand over his mouth but not before she saw his grin.

They arrived at the lockers, and a quick inspection revealed a couple of locks, but none of them appeared brand-new. Jordan must have chosen one in the men's locker room, which made a lot more sense than selecting a locker in plain sight. If Connor went to the locker room, Chaz might follow him, which would ruin any chance of finding and opening the right locker. Which meant she'd have to distract him.

"Do you have spin classes?" Brooke asked Chaz.

"Yes, we do."

"I love spinning!" she exclaimed, though she'd never been to a spin class in her life. "Connor doesn't like it, though. He's more into free weights."

Chaz ignored Connor and inched closer to Brooke. "I take our spin classes. It's a great cardio workout. Would you like to see the room where we hold them?"

"Totally!" Brooke said. Was that too enthusiastic? She noticed Connor rolling his eyes, but Chaz's attention was fixed on her. "If you don't mind showing me. I'd hate to take up too much of your time."

"No worries," Chaz said. "The room's this way."

He actually slipped a hand beneath her arm and guided her toward the front of the building. Connor followed. When they turned the corner behind the front desk, Brooke knew they were in the right place. The locker rooms were next to each other.

Connor evidently saw them too. "Do you mind if I use the facilities while you're checking out the spin room?"

Chaz didn't even bother to look at him. "Go ahead."

Connor glanced at her, then disappeared into the men's locker room.

Brooke followed Chaz into a glass-walled room filled with stationary bicycles. She focused all her attention on Chaz as he pointed out the cutting-edge features, high-definition touch screens, incline technology, and other options. She paid strict attention, as though she'd never had such a fascinating conversation, but out of the corner of her eye she watched the door to the locker room.

In less than two minutes, Connor appeared on the other side of the glass wall. He nodded at her and patted the pocket of his jeans.

She interrupted Chaz while he was telling her about the spin instructors. "Thank you for the tour, but we have to be going now." Without waiting for his reply, she spun on her heel and left the room.

Hustling to keep up with her, Chaz said, "Wait. You haven't seen everything yet. We have a tanning bed, massage chairs, and—"

"I'm sure they're great," Brooke said as she caught up with Connor. "But I just remembered we have an appointment, and we need to get going if we're going to make it in time."

Connor snapped his fingers. "I totally forgot too, honeybunch." He put a hand on the small of her back and guided her toward the exit.

"Let me know if you have any questions," Chaz called after them. "I can give you prices and so on."

They didn't bother to answer. Instead, they hurried out into the California sunshine and jumped into Brooke's car.

As soon as they were settled in their seats, she turned to him. "'Honeybunch'?"

He shrugged. "It seemed appropriate at the time."

"Whatever." Brooke waved an impatient hand. "Did you find the lock?"

"Sure did," Connor said. He wore a smug smile.

"Well?" she demanded. "What was in the locker?"

He reached into his pocket and then extended his hand. Resting in his palm was an object she recognized immediately.

A flash drive.

Brooke slid the key into the lock of her front door, then glanced over her shoulder at Connor. "Let me warn you. I have a killer cat."

"Yeah?" He cocked his head. "Like, he's feral or something?"

"Worse. He's a Siamese, and he hates men."

Connor raised a skeptical eyebrow.

"No, really," Brooke told him. "Sammy once launched an attack on a plumber who was trying to fix my garbage disposal. I used every bandage I had on the poor guy. He looked like a mummy when he left."

"He doesn't like men specifically?"

"He isn't crazy about strangers in general," Brooke answered. "He simply hides from women, but he attacks men. I adopted him from an animal shelter, so who knows what happened to him to make him that way." She unlocked the door. "The pizza delivery guy won't come to the door anymore. He stays in the car and calls me to come outside."

He cast a nervous glance at the door. "Maybe you should go in first and close him in a bedroom or something."

"And have him rip my quilt to shreds? No way." Brooke shrugged. "You don't have to come in. You could go home. I'll call you and tell you what's on the flash drive."

"Two problems with that plan," Connor said. "One, my car is in Skytech 1's parking lot. And two, I have a feeling I'll be waiting for a call that never comes."

She didn't meet his eye. He was right on both counts. Whatever Jordan had on that flash drive could have led to his death. Could she trust a journalist to keep whatever she found out of the newspaper? At the moment it seemed she would have to.

To her surprise, a sense of relief relaxed a nervous knot in the back of her neck. On some level she was glad Connor would be with her when she went through that flash drive. Maybe Sammy would behave himself for once. If he didn't, she had restocked her store of bandages.

"Watch yourself," Brooke warned as she opened the door.

Connor followed her inside, his head swiveling from side to side, likely searching for Sammy.

"He's probably sleeping in a window somewhere." She closed the door and tossed her keys on the table in the entry hall. "Come on. My computer's back here."

Brooke led him down the short hallway to her office and waved toward a spare chair while she circled the desk and booted up her computer.

Instead of sitting, he walked around the room, inspecting the pictures. "Is this your mother and father?" he asked, pointing to one.

"Stepfather," she corrected. "But yes, that's my mom."

"I can tell. You resemble her," Connor remarked, then moved on to the next, which was her diploma from UCLA. "Ah, I see you're local."

"I am now. I transferred my junior year. I grew up in Arizona."

"Do you mind if I get some water?" he asked.

"Help yourself," Brooke said, motioning in the direction of the kitchen. "Bottles are in the fridge."

Connor thanked her and left the room.

The monitor came to life, and she inserted the flash drive into an empty USB port. The drive opened to reveal about two hundred files. She paged through the list, noting the file types. They included spreadsheets, engineering schematics, programs, applications, images, and even a few blueprints. Her spirits sank. It would take forever to go through all of this.

Brooke sorted the list by descending date, and the document that came to the top was almost three years old. She opened it and recognized the proposal paper for the ten-drive stripe storage array project. After she joined the company, this was one of the first documents Jordan had given her to read in order to get a background on the groundbreaking project that he was convinced would revolutionize data storage.

She closed that file and opened the next, a cost analysis presented to Skytech 1's board of directors back when Jordan was trying to get them to sign off on risking a boatload of money. The project was estimated to run into the millions, and Brooke knew they'd exceeded that even before she was hired on.

Connor appeared in the doorway. "Is this the killer kitty you were talking about?"

Her jaw went slack. He held Sammy close to his chest in one hand and stroked the cat's white fur with the other. Sammy's blue eyes were closed to mere slits, and even across the room she could hear his contented purr.

"You were trying to get rid of me, weren't you?" Connor lowered his head and rubbed his cheek against Sammy's head. "This is the friendliest cat I've ever met."

"No, really." Brooke gawked at the pair of them, stunned. "He hates men."

"Well, he seems to like me." He tickled the cat's chin, then set him gently on the floor.

She watched as the feline began to twine around Connor's legs. "I've never seen Sammy do that to anyone except me."

Connor grinned. "He must be an excellent judge of character."

Brooke squinted at him suspiciously, trying to decide if he was bragging or complimenting her character. She shook her head and pointed at the monitor. "This is going to take awhile to review. There's a lot of data on here."

He came around to her side of the desk to stand beside her.

Connor was so close that she could have leaned over an inch and touched him. For some crazy reason, she had to fight an impulse to do precisely that. He smelled faintly of a musky aftershave that started a pleasant tickle in the pit of her stomach. She scooted in the opposite direction to put a safe distance between them.

"I recognize the spreadsheets and documents." Connor ran a finger down the list on the monitor. "But what are the rest of them?"

"Some are project management files." Brooke double-clicked on a file and scanned the list of tasks on the left side of a bar graph. "This dates back a couple of years. The tasks are mostly research and analysis."

He planted a hand on the desk and leaned toward the screen. "I can see it's a bar graph, but I have no idea what all those lines and colored blocks mean."

"It's basically a to-do list," she explained, "and the colors indicate who was assigned to perform each task."

"What color are you?"

"This was before I was hired." Brooke opened a different tab. "Blue is Jordan. The rest of the team are in different colors."

"Does anything jump out at you as significant?" Connor asked.

"Not really," she admitted. His nearness brought a fresh whiff of that distracting scent, and she was having a hard time concentrating.

Brooke closed the file and opened a spreadsheet containing the project budget, with expenditures detailed. It was around the same age as the graph.

"Whoever created this kept good records," Connor commented. "Even down to how much they spent on office supplies."

"That's good project management. This is a copy of a file we keep on a shared drive, where everyone can access it." Nothing in the list jumped out at her as noteworthy. Brooke closed the file and examined the list again. There were several other versions of the same spreadsheet, each with different dates. The newest was a few days old.

He stabbed a finger at the monitor. "I haven't seen this file type before."

"It's computer-aided design," she said. "We use that program to create blueprints."

"You made blueprints of this data storage project?"

"No, but we have blueprints of the facility that will manufacture the storage array. There's a prototype in Skytech 1's warehouse."

"That's important to the project, huh?" Connor asked.

"I guess," Brooke said, though her uncertainty was reflected in her voice. "The thing is, the R & D department doesn't create the blueprint files. I mean, I've seen them, but there's an entirely separate department of people who are proficient on that software."

"How does that work?"

"We tell them what's necessary to build the array. Then they create the blueprints, and the operations folks build the manufacturing equipment." She chewed on her bottom lip, thoughts whirling. "Why in the world would Jordan save older versions of the blueprints on a flash drive? And older versions of the budget? And the project plan?"

"Those files at the bottom are new," Connor pointed out.

"They are." The newest files were dated three days ago. The day before the failed test. These she recognized. The latest program code, project plan, blueprints, and budget.

"It's like Jordan made a copy of all the new files two days before he died," she said.

He kept studying the monitor. "All the new files?"

Brooke scanned the recent files again. Everything was there. Every file related to the storage array project. And every file was a duplicate of previous versions of the same information.

Connor straightened and peered at her. "You're thinking something. What is it?"

She gathered her thoughts. "Over the course of this project we've generated hundreds of thousands of files with data related to our project. But Jordan only copied about two hundred files onto this drive."

He voiced the question that niggled at her. "Why these files out of thousands?"

A possibility occurred to her. Brooke grabbed the mouse and re-sorted the list. A tiny ray of light illuminated an idea. "Look at this. If I were going to document all the important steps we've taken since the beginning of the project, these are the exact files that tell the story right up until now."

"So Jordan was showing the entire process."

She tapped on the monitor. "Yes, this is a complete history of the ten-drive stripe storage array. These files document the most critical elements of the project and every decision that impacted it from the start."

Connor folded his arms across his chest. "Why would he keep that kind of information on a flash drive? Doesn't the company back up data like this?"

"Yes, they do. And there's all kinds of security in place with the corporate data systems." She scanned the files. "He has the actual code for the array on this flash drive. That's highly confidential and proprietary information. It shouldn't be on an unsecured flash drive."

"Do you think Lancaster was doing something shady?"

Brooke couldn't believe that of Jordan. "He was honest and completely devoted to Skytech 1 and this project. I think he was keeping a backup of the critical data." She shook her head. "I don't know why. Maybe in case of a disaster?"

"Like an earthquake that destroyed the building and all the computers with it?" he suggested.

She didn't bother describing off-site storage and disaster recovery procedures. A physical disaster would cause a delay, but it wouldn't derail the project. "I think it's more likely he'd want a backup in case of something more sinister."

"Like what?"

Brooke met his gaze squarely. "Sabotage."

Mourners filed into the church for Jordan's funeral the following Monday.

Brooke sat in her car in the parking lot, battling a fit of nerves as she recognized many Skytech 1 employees. Did they know she'd been questioned by the police about Jordan's murder? Perhaps she shouldn't have come. But she wanted—no, needed—to support Holly. Brooke would have felt like a heel if she'd stayed home.

A knock on the car window startled her from her thoughts. She whirled around and saw Connor. What was he doing here? He didn't even know Jordan. Was he still chasing a story, hoping to get the inside scoop?

Remorse stabbed her. Connor had met Holly the other day. Maybe he merely wanted to show his support, the same as Brooke. She was starting to get a feel for the guy's character, and she didn't think he was the pushy reporter type she'd taken him for at first. Besides, Sammy liked him, and that Siamese cat hated almost everyone.

Brooke switched off the engine and opened the door. "I'm surprised to see you."

Connor held out a hand to assist her out of the car. "I knew you'd be here, and I figured you might appreciate some support."

A flash of irritation struck her. "I have plenty of friends. I'm sure they'll all be here."

But truth be told, she didn't have a lot of friends at work. And it would certainly feel better walking into the funeral with Connor by her side.

She smiled an apology for her sharp retort and took the proffered hand. "But thank you. I was just sitting here trying to get my nerve to go inside alone."

"Now you're not alone." His strong hand enveloped hers.

When she realized she'd held on to his hand a little longer than necessary, she jerked hers away and busied herself with locking the car and settling her purse strap on her shoulder.

They fell into an easy stride across the parking lot toward the church.

"I almost called you over the weekend," Connor said. "Did you find anything in those files?"

"No, I've gone through every one of them," Brooke replied, "and I didn't see anything out of the ordinary."

She was exhausted after spending the entire weekend at her computer, searching for clues. She'd stared at the screen so long that Sammy had taken matters into his own paws. He'd announced his displeasure by pouncing on the keyboard and batting his toys around her desk.

"On the other hand, I haven't had time to go over all the code in detail," Brooke continued. "That's my plan for the week. I'm going to run some comparisons and examine the changes from one file to the next. If nothing else, maybe I'll be able to figure out what happened to crash our test last week."

"I'm impressed. I wouldn't have the first idea how to begin something like that. I'm sure if anyone can figure it out, it's you."

Warmth crept up her neck, but she was saved from responding because at that moment they reached the church entrance.

They stepped inside, where a man in a dark suit greeted them in a hushed voice and directed them to sign the guest register. Soft music played from somewhere, and the scent of flowers saturated the air.

They entered the sanctuary, where the aroma was nearly overpowering. A riot of color covered the stage area. Rows of cushioned chairs, many of them occupied, faced the front of the room. A huge cross hung from the ceiling over a stage, where drums and an electronic keyboard sat. On each side of the cross were projection screens, blank at the moment. Though obviously a contemporary church, the overall feeling was one of quiet reverence.

But what drew her attention was the casket at the end of the center aisle. Thankfully the top was closed. Brooke was having enough trouble trying to erase the image of Jordan's body from her mind without having another vision of his corpse. She fervently hoped Holly hadn't seen him like that.

"Shall we pay our respects?" Connor whispered.

She glanced toward the front where Holly stood, flanked by her mother, one of her sisters, and a solemn-faced older couple who could only be Jordan's parents. A line of mourners waited to speak to them.

Brooke steeled herself, and together they headed down the aisle. Four people left chairs and stepped in front of them. Her R & D coworkers, dressed up for the funeral rather than in their usual jeans and polo shirts. Larry even wore a suit and tie.

"Hey," Roger said, studying her with a concerned expression. "You doing okay?"

"You seemed pretty upset when you left work," Derek said.

Greg scowled at him. "No wonder, doofus. You'd be upset too, wouldn't you?"

Because she'd been the one to find Jordan's body, or was he referring to something else? "What do you mean?" Brooke asked.

Derek lowered his voice. "They told us you're on administrative leave until the police investigation is over."

"It sounded like you're a suspect or something," Larry put in.

"Who said that?" Brooke asked faintly.

"Ed and Michael called us into a meeting after you left." Greg glanced at something behind her. "But we know that's a load of garbage."

She followed his gaze. Four rows behind them Mr. Harmon and Ed sat beside each other. Her gaze snagged on Ed's, and his nostrils flared before he pointedly averted his gaze. Mr. Harmon fixed his attention forward without making eye contact.

Connor slipped a hand beneath her arm. "We'd better move if we want to get a seat. The place is filling up." He guided her toward the front.

"I can't believe they're telling people I'm a murder suspect," she whispered, her mind reeling.

"Let it go," he said. "They'll have to eat their words when we uncover the truth."

They arrived at the front, and Holly caught sight of them. She excused herself to the man she was talking with and approached Brooke, her arms outstretched. "Thank you for coming."

Tears burned Brooke's eyes as she embraced the young widow. "I wish there was something I could say or do."

"I know." Holly pulled back and blotted her nose with a wadded tissue.

"How are you holding up?" Connor asked.

"As well as can be expected." Holly sniffed and glanced toward the haggard-looking couple standing beside the casket. "Better than Jordan's parents. They were supposed to fly here on Friday to watch Aria for the weekend while Jordan and I took a weekend getaway."

"A getaway?" Brooke asked.

"We were going to Mexico. He surprised me with it the morning he . . ." Holly gulped. "Well, it was going to be our first time leaving her and going away alone." She gave a shuddering breath. "Instead, we're saying goodbye to him forever."

Seeing Holly's raw anguish, Brooke felt her heart twist. "I'm so sorry," she managed to choke out past a lump the size of a mountain in her throat. This whole thing was such a nightmare and so unfair.

Holly got herself under control, then glanced around and lowered her voice. "Did you find the lock?"

"We did," Connor answered. "There was a flash drive in the locker."

"What's on it?" Holly asked.

"A bunch of files from work," Brooke told her. "I'm still trying to figure out what's so important that Jordan felt like he had to lock them up."

"I know you will," Holly said. She motioned to an elderly woman who was approaching. "Oh, there's Aunt Liza. I need to speak with her."

Brooke and Connor left Holly and found a seat near the back of the sanctuary.

"There's a lot of people here," Connor remarked when they'd settled into their chairs.

She glanced around the room. "A lot of them work at Skytech 1."

"I guess he was a popular guy."

Brooke frowned. Everyone seemed to be ignoring her. Not that she thought she deserved anyone's attention, but surely some people would acknowledge her presence by nodding a greeting or exchanging a sad gaze. Yet not a single person made eye contact with her. In fact, the more she tried to catch the eyes of her fellow employees, the more she became convinced that they were purposefully avoiding her. Some even gave her hard, disapproving looks.

Apparently gossip had been spreading in the office. Everyone thought she had killed Jordan. She slid down in her chair and hunched her shoulders, glad for Connor's presence.

At least someone didn't believe she was a murderer.

After the graveside service—sparsely attended compared to the funeral at the church—Brooke and Connor walked back to her car. A peaceful silence permeated the cemetery, and the only voices they heard were hushed murmurs.

"Do you want to grab a burger or something?" he asked when they arrived at her car.

Was that a request for a date? Brooke studied his guileless expression. It was impossible to tell, and she didn't want to embarrass herself by asking. "Thanks, but I think I'll go home and spend some more time trying to decipher those files."

Connor nodded. "Would it be okay if I call you tomorrow? To see if you've found anything in those files, I mean."

Though she still wasn't completely sure he could be trusted, she felt a little more accepting after seeing tears spill down his cheeks several times during the funeral service. And he had provided a strong supportive presence in an uncomfortable situation. She appreciated that. Besides, she needed someone to talk to if she wanted to figure out who killed Jordan.

The enormity of the task before her struck her anew. Brooke was trying to track down a killer. It wasn't from a sense of injustice or anything like that. She had to clear her name. In order to do that, she needed help from a trustworthy friend. Even though she'd just met him a few days ago under terrible circumstances, something inside her said Connor was someone she could trust.

"Sure," she said. "And if I find anything tonight, I'll give you a call."

A lopsided smile curved his lips. "Sounds good. Talk to you later."

During the drive home, she couldn't stop thinking about that smile.

When Brooke got home, Sammy met her at the door and yowled. She bent down and petted the cat. "I'll bet you're angling for a treat."

Sammy purred and rubbed against her legs.

Brooke smiled as she went to the kitchen. After setting her purse and phone on the counter, she retrieved the bag of treats and dropped a few into his bowl.

Sammy devoured them.

Over the next few hours, Brooke pored over computer code, searching for anything out of order. She'd seen it a dozen times, and everything appeared perfectly normal. Finally, her vision started to blur, and she rocked back in her desk chair, blinking hard.

Her cell phone rang from the kitchen. Was it Connor? She was too tired to talk right now, and she had nothing to report. She decided to let the call go to voice mail.

There was silence, and then the phone rang a second time.

Admitting defeat, she trotted into the kitchen. She snatched the phone off the counter and glanced at the screen. It was Holly Lancaster. Brooke answered. "Is everything okay?"

"No!" The voice on the other end choked with suppressed sobs. "We got home from the funeral, and the house has been broken into."

"Oh no," Brooke said. "I'm so sorry."

"They ransacked Jordan's office," Holly sobbed. "Drawers upended and files thrown everywhere."

Brooke sank against the counter, her knees suddenly weak. The description sounded very much like the disaster she'd found in Jordan's office at work. The killer must have been searching for something specific. Like a flash drive?

"What can I do to help?" Brooke asked.

"Could you come over? I think it must be related to Jordan's death," Holly said, a hint of rage in her tone. "His laptop is gone."

10

"I can't believe this." Holly sat on her sofa, hugging a throw pillow with a dazed expression. "It's like a nightmare that keeps going."

Mary, Holly's sister, sat close to her, a protective arm around her shoulders, sharing Holly's misery and serving as a solid support in the storm that had torn her sister's life apart.

Brooke perched on the edge of a facing chair, feeling more helpless than she ever had in her life. Through the patio doors sunshine sparkled on the surface of the pool, and the fronds of an ornamental palm stirred in a slight breeze. It was a tranquil scene at complete odds with the chaos inside the house. The front door stood open, and a string of police officers came and went through it. She recognized some of them from the murder scene at Skytech 1 and avoided meeting their eyes.

In the living room there was minimal evidence of the theft. An empty shelf in the entertainment center where a video game console used to be. A broken ornamental vase. A few books scattered on the floor. The television was still mounted on the wall, the giant flat screen apparently too big for the thieves to take.

Jordan's office, however, had been the focus of the theft. Brooke had glanced in there when she'd arrived. If possible, it was an even bigger mess than the one at Skytech 1. Only without the body, thank goodness.

Now she could hear the officers' low and indistinct voices coming from the office and see the glow from the occasional camera flash.

"Where's Aria?" Brooke asked, mostly to break the awful silence in the living room.

"Our mom took her," Mary said. "We thought it was better to get her out of the house."

"Of course she doesn't understand what's going on," Holly whispered. "She keeps going from room to room asking for Daddy. And you know what? A couple of times I've found myself doing the same." Her face crumpled, and she buried her head in the pillow.

Mary rested her forehead on her sister's shoulder and cried silent, sympathetic tears.

A familiar figure stepped through the front door. "I came as fast as I could," Connor said.

A rush of relief brought Brooke to her feet. His strong and reassuring presence lightened some of the tightness in her chest. She hurried across the room and stopped herself a second before opening her arms for a hug. Embarrassed for her show of familiarity, she wrapped her arms around herself and smiled. "Thanks for coming."

"Of course," he said softly, with a warm smile just for her. Then his gaze moved to Holly. "I'm so sorry this is happening to you. Is there anything I can do?"

With a visible effort, Holly composed herself. "If you have a magic wand to wave and erase the past few days, that would be great."

"I'm fresh out of magic wands," Connor said with understanding and regret. "But you have my prayers, if that helps."

Holly gave him a sad but grateful smile. "It helps. Thank you."

Another figure stomped into the room. That was the only way to describe Detective Travis's stride, as though he were arriving at a brush fire and was prepared to smother it single-handedly.

Brooke shrank inwardly, took an unconscious step toward Connor, and avoided looking directly at the detective.

When Travis spied Holly, his features and his tread softened. "My condolences. Rest assured we will find the culprits involved and recover your stolen belongings."

Holly's brow creased. "Thank you. But TVs and game consoles are merely possessions. You can never give me back the one thing that matters most to me." Her lips trembled. "My husband."

A thought occurred to Brooke. Before she could stop herself, she blurted, "Nothing will bring Jordan back, but finding the person responsible will make us all rest easier." She gestured toward the ransacked office. "And now you'll have some new evidence to go on."

Travis turned slowly toward her, an icy smile on his lips. "How interesting to find you here. I wish I could say I'm surprised."

Brooke bristled. What did he mean by that?

"Brooke is here at my request," Holly told him.

"Is that so?" Travis continued to hold Brooke's gaze, though he spoke to Holly. "Why would you request the presence of one of your late husband's employees? I was given to believe that the two of you had little or no personal connection."

On the sofa Holly sat up a little taller. "That was true last week, but circumstances have changed, haven't they?"

Brooke tore her gaze away from Travis to give Holly a grateful look.

Connor took a sidestep that brought him close enough to Brooke that their arms touched.

The comfort that contact brought served to bolster her confidence, and Brooke was able to meet the detective's eye without flinching.

"They have indeed." Travis returned his attention to Holly. "As I was saying, I'm sorry this tragedy has come so quickly after the first. I'm afraid it isn't unheard of for robberies to occur as a family mourns a loss."

"What do you mean?" Holly asked.

The detective splayed his hands. "Unscrupulous people scour the newspapers and the Internet for local obituaries. They make note of service times, when they know the family will be otherwise occupied, and that's when they strike."

"You can't believe this robbery is random," Brooke said, unable to hold her tongue. "That it isn't related to the murder."

"I don't believe anything at this point," Travis said sharply. "But we have to consider every option. I admit it's not likely, but we can't ignore the possibility that the two separate crimes were committed by two separate criminals."

"Feel free to see yourself to Jordan's office." Holly motioned toward the short hallway. "That's where they spent all their time. And they took my husband's computer. Isn't that evidence?"

The detective pulled his cell phone from his pocket and read from the screen. "With all due respect, they also took a gaming console, a jar containing approximately $120 in change, and a flat-screen television." He glanced at the big one hanging on the wall.

"The one in our bedroom," Holly clarified.

"Also a baby monitoring system," Travis finished.

"The jerks," Connor mumbled.

Brooke leaned toward him so their arms rested against each other.

"But they left two tablets," Holly said. "They were sitting right out in the open."

"They were probably equipped with GPS, which would make them easy to track," Travis pointed out. "No, this sounds like the perpetrator knew what he was doing, and he had done it before."

Holly shook her head. "But—"

Travis raised a hand, cutting her off. "Please don't think I'm dismissing the possibility that the murderer and the thief are the same person. Rest assured that the LAPD will investigate every angle. For instance . . ." He whirled toward Brooke. "Where were you today?"

Taken off guard, Brooke felt her heart skip a beat. "When Holly called, I was at home."

Holly stood, and the pillow in her lap dropped to the floor. She crossed the room to stand beside Brooke. "She attended my husband's funeral, and she also came to the graveside service. There is no way Brooke could have done this. I wish you would stop focusing on her, because the real killer is still out there."

Flanked by Connor and Holly, Brooke straightened her shoulders and stood a little taller.

Travis still reminded her of an iceberg, but he did incline his head slightly to acknowledge Holly's defense. Then he turned to Connor. "And what about you? What are you doing here?"

Connor slipped his hand into Brooke's, and his warm fingers intertwined with hers.

A rush of emotion washed over her from her head to her toes.

Connor smiled at the detective. "Moral support."

After a long moment, Travis snorted. Without another word, he spun on his heel and marched toward the ransacked office.

Connor took four glasses out of the cabinet and set them on the spotless granite countertop in Holly's kitchen.

Brooke hunted in the fridge for something to tempt Holly's appetite. The widow and Mary sat at the kitchen table with their hands clasped in mutual comfort. Holly bore a hollow, haunted look that stirred something deep in Connor's heart.

Brooke emerged with a tray covered in plastic wrap. "Refreshments, anyone?"

The tray held an assortment of deli pinwheels and a selection of fresh vegetables. The fridge was full of similar items, traditional offerings for a grieving family.

"I'm not hungry," Holly answered in a wooden voice.

"You're going to eat," Mary told her, then waved at Brooke to bring the tray to the table. "Aria needs her mother to stay strong and healthy."

Connor nodded. He thought it was the right thing to say.

Brooke set the tray in the center of the table, along with a stack of small paper plates. Holly picked up a cherry tomato and put it on a plate, and Mary immediately and sternly added two pinwheels and some baby carrots.

Connor filled the glasses with ice and water and joined the three ladies at the table. Though he wasn't hungry, he helped himself to some food, as did Brooke and Mary. *Companionable eating*, his mother called it. If they all sat there and stared at Holly, she wouldn't touch a bite. But if she saw them eating, maybe she would follow suit without even realizing it.

"Thank you." The shadow of a smile crept to Holly's lips as she cast a grateful glance around the table. Her gaze came to rest on Brooke. "I'm so sorry you got pulled into this mess. I'm afraid I've only made things worse by calling you about the lock."

Brooke shook her head, and a dark curl brushed her cheek. "Don't apologize. I'm glad you did, though I have to admit I'm not sure I'll be able to figure out what was so important that Jordan felt the need to hide it."

"Maybe you should give it to the police after all." Holly jerked her head toward the office, where Detective Travis's voice could be heard barking instructions to the officers gathering evidence.

"I'll have to eventually," Brooke said, her expression troubled. "I just wish I could tell him why all those files are so important."

Connor curled his fingers around hers. The gesture was meant to offer her comfort, but a pleasant warmth spread up his arm from the contact, and he found he didn't want to let go. Nor, he realized with a thrill, did she pull away.

Advancing footsteps alerted them to the approach of Detective Travis a moment before he appeared in the kitchen doorway.

Brooke snatched her hand away.

With a sting of regret, Connor rested his hand on the table.

"We're all finished in there," the detective told Holly. "Officer Ruiz has some papers for you to sign. A list of the missing items and so on."

A uniformed officer entered the kitchen and approached the table. Holly pushed her plate out of the way, and Ruiz set a stack of papers in front of her.

Travis fixed a gaze on Brooke. "May I speak with you for a moment?" He left the room without waiting for an answer.

She jerked upright, her face draining of color, and glanced at Connor.

He interpreted her look as a plea for help. Rising, he scooted his chair beneath the table and held out a hand to her. The gratitude in those beautiful green eyes as she took his hand washed through him.

Together they followed the detective into the living room.

Travis's gaze dropped to take in their clasped hands. "I'd like to speak to Ms. Lester alone," he told Connor with obvious disapproval.

Brooke tightened her grip on his hand.

Connor met the detective's sternness with a smile. "She's had an emotional day, and she really needs a friend to stay with her, if you don't mind."

The detective smirked. "Providing moral support?"

"Exactly."

"Very well." Travis focused on Brooke. "I hope you realize we haven't dismissed the evidence of the security video and the badge records, even though it appears you weren't involved in any criminal activity today." He waved toward the office. "At least, you weren't personally involved."

"What do you mean?" Her voice wavered on the last word.

"It is abundantly clear that you are somehow involved in Mr. Lancaster's murder."

She opened her mouth to protest.

But Travis stopped her by holding up a finger. "We're investigating every possibility, including the fact that you may have been victimized by an unscrupulous person you consider a friend."

"A friend?" Confusion showed on Brooke's furrowed brow. "Who?"

"I have no idea," Travis said. "But if you'll take some advice, you may want to exercise a little caution in choosing your companions." He gestured at Connor. "This one, for instance."

A rod of steel slid into Connor's spine. What was the man getting at?

Beside him, Brooke gazed at him with silent questions.

Connor shrugged. "I don't know what he means."

"I think you do," Travis said. "You see, I have a buddy from my police academy days who works for the Ohio State Highway Patrol. And I happened to be talking to him the other day. You're from Ohio, aren't you?"

Cold dread settled into his stomach. "I am."

Travis started toward the front door, speaking over his shoulder as he went. "That's what I heard. If you're so determined to help Ms. Lester, maybe you should stop lying to her. Perhaps you should tell her about your history of criminal activity."

"Wait!" Connor called to Brooke as she sprinted toward her car. He matched her pace and raced through the Lancasters' manicured front lawn.

Desperate to get away from him, Brooke dodged sideways around the Toyota's rear bumper and dashed a traitorous tear out of her eye. "Leave me alone!" she cried, fumbling in her purse. Why did her keys always end up in the bottom of her purse beneath a jumble of junk?

"But I can explain," Connor said, coming to a stop at her side.

"I don't want to hear any excuses." She sniffed and wiped her eyes with her sleeve.

"It's not an excuse," he insisted. "It's an explanation."

Brooke finally grasped the key fob and pulled the keys out. Pointing the fob toward the car, she pressed a button to unlock the doors.

Instead, the trunk clicked open.

"Stupid thing!" A sob choked her voice. She ran to the rear and slammed the trunk. Twin tears splashed onto the blue paint.

"Please listen to me," Connor said. He reached out and caught her hand.

His touch halted her. Brooke glared at the hand she'd drawn comfort from only moments ago. But that comfort had been false. She jerked her hand away. "You lied to me."

"I did not!"

Whirling around, she sidestepped him, punching the unlock button as she did. The right button this time.

He dashed in front of her and stood with his back to the door, blocking her way. "Listen to me." Something rang in his tone, giving the words an extraordinary impact. "I don't lie. I never lie. You can bank on that."

The determination in his eyes and the firm set of his jaw tempted her to believe him.

"What did I lie about?" Connor tossed the question out like a challenge. "I told you the minute you asked that I was a journalist. Truth. I told you I would keep everything you say out of the paper until we figure this out. Again, truth. I haven't mentioned the lock, the flash drive, the files, or anything we've uncovered to a single soul except you."

What he said was true. Sifting back through their conversations, Brooke couldn't pinpoint a single untrue statement he'd made. Why did she feel so hurt? So betrayed?

Because I trusted him, and he took advantage of me to get an exclusive on this story.

"Not telling the whole truth is the same thing as a lie," Brooke said, but her voice lacked conviction.

"Then give me the chance to tell you the truth," Connor said. "When I'm done, you can be the judge about whether or not I've purposefully deceived you."

Brooke remained silent as she considered it. Part of her wanted to tell him to get lost. She didn't need him or any other guy manipulating her for their own benefit. But he had helped her find the flash drive, and he'd gone with her to Jordan's funeral. The tears she'd seen there hadn't been fake. They were tears of sorrow for a young widow's tragedy and a little girl's lost father.

Heaving a sigh, she crossed her arms over her chest. "Okay, go ahead and explain."

"Not here," he said, scanning the area.

Brooke followed his gaze. She noticed a neighbor across the street watching them, children playing in a nearby yard, and a woman walking her dog. If Travis was right and Connor was about to unveil his criminal past, she couldn't blame him for not wanting to spill his guts on a public street.

"There's a coffee shop a couple of blocks away," he suggested.

Was she ready to trust him? Was it a good idea to hop into his car and let him drive her? He could take her anywhere, and she'd be trapped.

"I'll follow you," she said.

Connor picked up the two lattes from the barista and headed for the corner table where Brooke sat stiffly, holding tightly to the purse in her lap as if she expected him to snatch it out of her hands and make a run for it.

A stab of irritation at Detective Travis set his teeth together. All of Connor's instincts told him Brooke was cautious when it came to relationships, especially with men. Something had happened to make her that way, and he hoped to gain enough of her trust to confide in him. To maybe break through that protective barrier she'd built. And he'd been making headway until Travis dropped the bomb that could have destroyed everything. Cops should stick to the business of enforcing the law and not meddle in other people's lives.

"There you go." He set a cup in front of her. "Skinny coconut latte, hold the whip."

"Thank you." She didn't meet his eye, but she released the grip on her purse long enough to pick up the cup and take a sip. "It's good."

Connor pulled out the chair across from her and slid closer to the table. He took a sip from his cup, but his taste buds had gone on strike. On the drive here, he'd tried to come up with the best approach to explain his past to the beautiful woman across from him.

When he opened his mouth, his plan dissolved. "That detective lied," he said flatly.

Disbelief was evident on her features.

"No, really," Connor insisted. Then he drew a breath and gathered his thoughts. "At least, he didn't tell the whole story. I was thirteen years old. A buddy and I were just starting to flirt with trouble, like most teenagers do."

As he said it, the thought occurred to him that maybe Brooke hadn't been like most teenagers. Maybe she'd never gotten into trouble or taken risks. She'd probably been a good girl her whole life, the class brain who stayed at home every night to study.

Connor gulped a mouthful of scalding coffee. "So we were hanging out at his house one night. You know, having a sleepover. And we were playing this awful video game where you basically score points for committing crimes."

Brooke didn't say anything as she watched him.

Suddenly he had a hard time looking at her, so he wrapped his hands around his cup and focused on the plastic top. "So it was about three in the morning, and my buddy said he knew where his dad kept the keys to his Corvette."

From the corner of his eye, he saw her wince. Encouraged, he continued. "Yeah, we were stupid kids. We took the Corvette out for a joyride. But here's the thing. Marietta, Ohio, isn't a big town. Everybody knew who owned that car."

Finally, she broke her silence. "A neighbor ratted you out?"

Connor laughed. "More like five of them. Who knew the people of Marietta stayed up all night? We hadn't gotten three miles before the police pulled us over, and it wasn't long before my buddy's dad got there." All these years later, the memory was as vivid as if it had happened yesterday. "My dad was right behind him."

"That must have been awful," Brooke commented.

He noticed that her shoulders had relaxed. And was that a trace of sympathy he detected? "Trust me. It was. Thank goodness the cops stopped us before we crashed the car or caused any damage. The judge took that into account when he found us guilty."

"Ouch," she said.

Connor could still conjure the image of the severe Judge McAfee, and he could still hear the sound of that gavel crashing down. "Ouch is right. We both got community service, and my dad added his own penalty. I had to detail cars for a local car dealer and give every bit of the money to the church. Even the tips."

A smile twitched at the corners of her lips. "Did you learn your lesson?"

"Yes ma'am," he assured her with a grin. Then he sobered. "Here's the thing. I was thirteen. From that point on, I have a spotless record. Not even a speeding ticket. And I had my juvenile record expunged when I was eighteen. It doesn't exist anymore, so Detective Travis's friend must have remembered when it happened."

Brooke leaned back in the chair. Sometime during his story she had set her purse on the floor, and now she cupped her latte with fingers that showed no evidence of the anger or resentment he'd sensed when they first arrived. Thank goodness for that.

"I wonder what made Detective Travis call his old friend to check up on you." The remark sounded more like a thought she was pondering.

"I've been wondering about that too." Connor leaned forward across the table and held her gaze. "The only reason I can think of is that he wanted to dig up something that would make you mistrust me. He's trying to drive a wedge between us. But why?"

She remained silent, apparently pondering his question.

He held his breath, waiting for her to come to whatever conclusion seemed logical to her and hoping beyond hope she decided in his favor.

"Travis must want to keep me uncertain and alone," Brooke said at last. "He isn't sure I'm the killer, but he is attempting to cover all his bases. If I have no one in my corner, I'm more vulnerable. But with friends, I'm stronger."

That was the opening Connor was waiting for. He rested his arm on the table, palm up. "I'm your friend. Will you trust me?"

He didn't breathe for several seconds while she considered. Then she took his hand. The spark in the green eyes that caught his lit a flame inside him.

She smiled. "I trust you."

The next morning, Brooke woke up to the sound of Sammy's chirping purr. She checked the time and groaned. It was six o'clock.

"Why didn't you let me sleep in?" she asked the cat.

Sammy rubbed his head against her arm.

With a sigh, Brooke padded to the kitchen with the cat on her heels. After feeding Sammy and freshening his water bowl, she poured a cup of coffee and leaned against the counter, wondering what to do with her day. She needed to continue studying the files on the flash drive, but she wasn't up to the task right now. Her mind was still too cloudy.

She took her cup of coffee to the living room and sat down on the couch. Brooke hadn't been without a job since her junior year in high school, and she struggled to think of something to fill the empty hours.

Sammy joined her on the sofa. He curled up on her lap and fell asleep almost immediately.

As Brooke stroked the sleeping cat, she considered the events of the previous day. It had been difficult attending Jordan's funeral, but Connor had certainly helped her through it. He'd also helped her through the aftermath of the break-in at Holly's and the detective's accusations. The fact that Travis had attempted to destroy her trust in Connor made her angry.

She pushed away the distressing thoughts and flipped on the television, but it was too lame to be endured. Then she picked up a book, but she couldn't concentrate. At this rate, the hours would drag by at a snail's pace. She decided the only thing left to do was clean the house from top to bottom again.

Sammy took refuge on top of the curtain rod in the living room. From his vantage point, he warily watched her pace from room to room.

By lunchtime, not a single speck of dust could be found anywhere in the house, her closets would have passed a military inspection with flying colors, and her kitchen cabinets had been reorganized—twice.

Brooke grabbed a sandwich and a glass of iced tea, then retreated to her office. Before she could get to work, the phone rang. She checked the screen. It was Connor.

"How are you doing today?" he asked.

"I'm fine," she said. "But Sammy wouldn't let me sleep in."

"Of course not," Connor said with a laugh. "Have you found anything in the files yet?"

"I'm getting ready to dive into them again."

"Are you busy this evening? I could bring dinner."

Brooke wanted to decline his offer, but she realized that she could use the company. "Sure. It sounds nice."

"Great," he said. "I'd better get back to work."

They settled on a time, then disconnected.

For the rest of the afternoon, Brooke scrutinized the files, becoming more and more frustrated. She had to figure this out. But how?

Finally, she gave up. But now she faced her earlier problem again. She had nothing to do. The house was already clean, and reading and watching TV still didn't appeal to her.

When the doorbell rang at seven, she was so relieved to have a visitor that she rushed to the door.

Connor stood there with a pizza in one hand and a bag of cat treats in the other.

Brooke let him into the house, irritated by a rush of pleasure at the sight of his crooked grin. The reason she was happy to see him was because she was bored to tears, nothing else.

Sammy dashed to greet his apparent best friend. He begged for affection and twined around Connor's legs, purring.

She shook her head. The traitor.

"What's wrong?" Connor asked after giving the cat his due. "You're scowling."

"Am I?" Brooke forced her facial muscles to relax, then eyed the pizza box. "What toppings did you get?"

"Pineapple and ham." A shadow crossed his features. "I hope that's okay. It's my favorite."

Actually, those were Brooke's favorite toppings too, but she didn't say so. She turned and closed the door to hide her expression. "I'm good with whatever."

In the kitchen Connor fed a delighted Sammy treats while Brooke put plates and napkins on the dinette table.

When they'd seated themselves across from each other and helped themselves to the food, Connor asked, "Any progress today?"

She scowled again. "None. I've pored over those files for days, and I still have no idea what Jordan was doing with them."

"Maybe you're trying too hard. You should take a break." He picked off a pineapple and popped it into his mouth.

Brooke poked at her pizza with a fork. "There's a killer out there somewhere who's trying to frame me for murder, and a police detective who is only too happy to believe the worst. I can't take a break." She winced at the sharpness in her tone and flashed him an apologetic smile. "Sorry."

Connor waved off the apology. "No worries. It's understandable that you're stressed. But it's possible you're missing something in those files because you've been looking so hard at them. If you step away for a day or so, you can come back to them refreshed and able to consider new angles. Maybe something will jump out at you."

"You're probably right, but I can't focus on anything else." She tossed her fork on the table. "That flash drive is consuming my every thought and keeping me awake at night."

"You need a distraction."

"Like what?"

He finished his slice of pizza. "Like going to the beach or to dinner or both." He bit his lip, then blurted, "With me."

A thrill zipped down her spine. With an effort, she kept her tone even. "Are you asking me on a date?"

"You don't have to think of it as a date if you don't want to," Connor said. "You could view it as a diversionary tactic to help clear your mind."

Brooke stared at him, thoughts spinning. Actually, the notion of a date with Connor wasn't as terrible today as it would have been last week. In fact, she found the idea kind of appealing, and that bothered her. A lot. She couldn't pinpoint why, and she didn't want to think about it. But a few hours at the beach and a relaxing dinner would get her out of the house and give her something to focus on besides computer code and manufacturing schematics.

"Tomorrow," she said and was deeply gratified by the sight of his lopsided grin.

Brooke ran a brush through her hair and examined herself in the mirror. A little makeup would give her some color, but who put on makeup to go to the beach? As soon as the first salty wave hit, she would be a mess, with running mascara and water dripping from her hair onto her shoulders. Not exactly attractive.

The doorbell rang. Connor was early.

With a final glance at her image, she snatched up a hair elastic and pulled the dark mass into a ponytail at the back of her head on her way to the door. As she grabbed the handle and opened the door, she said, "Are you always—"

Surprise snatched the question out of her mouth. Instead of Connor, Derek Ingram was on her front stoop. What was he doing here? How did he even know where she lived? She wondered if he had followed her home from work.

The systems programmer stood with his arms hanging awkwardly at his sides. Derek didn't quite meet her gaze, but he seemed to focus instead on her chin. "I had to run an errand not far from here, and I thought I'd stop by and see how you're doing. I hope that's okay."

Brooke was so stunned that she didn't reply at first. Why would he give her a second thought? She and Derek weren't friends. They weren't even friendly coworkers. He'd always been kind of a loner and had never struck her as being particularly thoughtful of others. "Thanks. That's nice of you."

He shifted his gaze to the top of her head. "So, can I come in? I won't stay long."

Her first instinct was to say no. But that would be rude. Besides, maybe something had happened at work that he wanted to tell her about. News about the project or even about Jordan's death.

Brooke gave in to curiosity and stepped aside to let him in. "Of course."

Derek sidled past her and stood in the middle of the living room, examining his surroundings.

She closed the door. "Can I get you something to drink?"

"No thanks," he said. "I'm good."

An uncomfortable silence descended, broken by an angry hiss.

Derek jerked toward the sound.

Sammy stood in the doorway to the kitchen, his back arched, and glared at the newcomer.

"Don't mind him. He's cranky." Brooke hurried to pick up the cat before he attacked her guest. "Have a seat. I'll be right back."

After Sammy had been closed in the bathroom with a stern admonishment to behave himself, she returned to find Derek perched on the edge of her sofa.

She settled in the matching chair and watched him. When he said nothing, she asked, "So how are things at the office?"

"Quiet." He clasped his hands between his knees. "It's still hard to believe Jordan is gone."

The comment sounded wooden, like something he'd repeated often. Which was probably the case.

Derek began to bounce one heel on the carpet while he scanned the room as though searching for something to say.

As far as Brooke knew, they had nothing in common except work. "How's the project going?"

His chest heaved with a disdainful blast of air. "Ed has stepped in as the project manager, but he's no Jordan. Things have pretty much stalled."

No surprise there. Ed wasn't the roll-up-your-sleeves type. "That's a shame."

"Yeah." Derek bit his lip. "So, there's some talk going around the office."

Now the reason for this visit was obvious. The rumor mill was in full operation, and he'd come here to get the scoop directly from the subject of the gossip.

"Really?" she asked, allowing a cool tone to creep into her voice. "What kind of talk?"

"They're saying you killed Jordan." For the first time he looked her in the eye. "They say there's security footage of you coming in really early that morning and something about your badge."

Thanks to Rick in security, no doubt. Or maybe even Ed. "Is that right?"

"Most people don't believe you're the kind of person who would kill someone. I mean, I don't. That recording has to be doctored or something."

It was a nice thing to say, but something about his manner kept her nerves on alert. Was he trying to manipulate her by making her think he was on her side?

Brooke acknowledged the show of support with a nod. "Thank you."

"It's just—" Derek broke off, and his gaze became intense. "Someone sure went to a lot of trouble to make it seem like you did it."

"That's what I told the police," she said.

"But why you?" he continued. "Why would they try to frame the least likely person in the department?"

Though glad he thought she was an unlikely murderer, Brooke tensed. Something about the way he was watching her put her on edge. "I wish I knew the answer to that."

Derek propped his elbows on his knees and leaned toward her. "Did you and Jordan know each other personally? Like, outside of work?"

Caution flags rose in her mind. These questions came too close to the ones Detective Travis had asked over and over when he was interrogating her. "What do you mean?"

"Everybody knew he liked you. It was obvious. He was always asking your opinion and assigning you the best tasks, the ones we all wanted."

Her spine became rigid. "That's not true."

"Sure it is. We all noticed."

His manner had become more what she was accustomed to seeing from him—arrogant, jealous, and slightly superior. As if he knew something she didn't, something that gave him an advantage over her.

A new emotion wormed its way into her mind. Someone had impersonated her for the security recording, someone around her size. Derek stood just a few inches taller, which would have been impossible to detect from the downward-facing angle of the camera, especially if he hunched over. He was as thin as a beanpole, and he probably weighed only slightly more than she did. The person on the camera had camouflaged their build with a bulky jacket. Had it been Derek?

And if Derek had killed Jordan, why was he here today? Was he planning to hurt her, maybe even kill her too?

The doorbell rang.

The sudden sound unglued her from her chair. Brooke leaped to her feet and dashed across the room to open the door.

Connor stood on the stoop, smiling at her.

Relief wilted her tense muscles, and it took all her power not to fling her arms around him. "I'm so glad you're here. Come in." She grabbed his arm and hauled him into the house.

Clearly surprised by her exuberant greeting, Connor opened his mouth to say something and then caught sight of Derek, who had risen from the couch and stood with his arms hanging at his sides.

Brooke shut the door, but she kept her hold on Connor's arm. "Do you remember Derek Ingram? You two met at the funeral."

"Coworker, right?" Connor extended his free hand.

"Yes." Derek shook the proffered hand, but he jerked away abruptly.

Brooke forced herself to release Connor's arm, but she continued to hover close to his side. "Connor works for a newspaper."

The programmer's eyes went round. "You're a reporter?"

A tiny sigh escaped from Connor, and he responded in a resigned tone, "Something like that."

"That's, uh, cool." Derek's throat bobbed nervously. He took a step toward the door. "So I'm glad you're doing okay," he told Brooke. "I need to get going."

Though relieved that the visit was at an end, she couldn't help but wonder at the speed with which Derek left the house.

When the door shut behind him, Connor pulled the edge of the curtain back and peeked outside. "Was it something I said?"

Brooke sank into the chair, her limp arms hanging over the sides. "That was the strangest conversation I've ever had. He showed up out of the blue with some lame excuse about checking on me, then told me that everyone at work thinks I killed Jordan."

Connor winced. "Sorry about that."

She waved the sympathy away. "That didn't surprise me at all. But he started insinuating that Jordan and I were somehow involved. Then things got kind of weird."

He cocked his head. "How so?"

Brooke took a moment to choose her words. "He said someone went to a lot of trouble to point the blame at me. I know it sounds strange, but the way he was watching me gave me the creeps. Like he was sizing me up or something. And then I realized he isn't that much taller or heavier than me."

"You think he dressed up like you, hacked your badge number, and killed your boss?"

Before today she wouldn't have thought Derek Ingram capable of doing serious harm to anyone. But why else would he show up at her house? What was behind the ridiculous accusation about her and Jordan?

Finally, she shook her head. "I wish I knew."

"Has he been here before?"

Brooke snorted. "No. I keep my career separate from my personal life."

"Then how did he know where you live?" Connor asked. "Did he follow you from work at some point?"

The thought had occurred to her briefly when she opened the door to find Derek on her stoop. "The departmental directory has our phone numbers but nothing else. On the other hand, with my cell phone number and my full name, he could have easily found me on the Internet." She frowned. "You'd be surprised how much personal information is available on the Internet if you know where to search for it."

"So he would have had to make an effort to find you," Connor said. She nodded.

He paced from the window to the sofa, his expression thoughtful. "How many people at work could put on a loose jacket and carry a purse like yours and actually pass for you?"

A humorless laugh escaped her lips. "About five hundred."

"Good point," Connor said. "But think about the people your boss interacted with on a regular basis. His coworkers, employees, people like that."

A series of images rose before her. Ed Gentry, the director, was short and stocky. Even in a bulky jacket, there was no way he'd resemble the person she'd seen on that security footage. Jordan had regularly reported progress of the company's key project to several of the executives, including the CEO. Every female she could think of was heavier or shaped differently enough that she dismissed them. Nor did any of the men fit the bill.

In the R & D department there were only the five of them. Larry outweighed her by at least fifty pounds, so that ruled him out. Greg, Roger, and Derek were all of average height and build, so she supposed any of them could be a likely candidate.

"I wish I could see that security recording again," Brooke said. "I was so shocked when I saw it that I didn't pay close enough attention to features that could prove it wasn't me."

"A lawyer could probably subpoena a copy of it," he said.

She jerked upright. "Do you think I need a lawyer?"

"I don't know," Connor admitted. "You haven't been charged with anything, but it might not hurt to have an attorney's number ready to call in case you end up needing one."

Even though the advice was good, it left her feeling a little sick to her stomach. Brooke made a mental note to do some research on good defense attorneys.

A feline yowl resounded down the hallway.

"Did you lock Sammy up?" he asked.

She detected a hint of accusation in Connor's tone. "I had to," she said more defensively than she intended. "He was about to attack Derek."

"You should have let him." He paced down the hallway and returned with Sammy in his arms. "You remember what I said about this cat being an excellent judge of character?"

She gave a wry smile. "Yes."

"Maybe you should listen to him. He might have identified a killer."

Connor escorted Brooke to her front door that night.

The sun had set over the Pacific half an hour ago while they drove along the highway with the salt-scented air blowing in their faces. Shadows hid most of Brooke's neighborhood, broken by bright circles from the neighbors' porch lights. She hadn't left her porch light on, but a light breeze blew clouds across the moon's surface, bathing them in a periodic white glow.

"I had a good time," Brooke said.

They'd spent the afternoon at Malibu Beach, bodysurfing, swimming, and building a sandcastle so huge that passersby stopped to take pictures of it. Then they'd gone up the coast in the Mustang with the top down. She'd stopped worrying about her salt-encrusted, windblown hair after the first mile and let it fly behind her like a tail.

An early dinner followed on the patio of a roadside fish shack that served the best chowder she'd ever tasted. For several hours, she had managed to forget about Jordan, Detective Travis, and the mystery of the flash drive.

Connor smiled. "I did too."

The skin on his cheeks and across the bridge of his nose shone bright red. Without thinking, Brooke lifted her hand and touched his nose with a finger.

"Ouch." He jerked his head out of reach.

She chuckled. "I told you to put on more sunscreen."

Frowning, Connor pressed the burned skin gingerly with his own finger. "It was supposed to be waterproof."

"Well, I'd better get inside," Brooke said, fishing her key out of her purse.

"If you follow my advice, you'll take a long bath and go to bed. Start fresh in the morning." He cocked his head, a smile toying with his lips. "But you're not going to do that."

"I'm not?"

"As soon as I leave, you'll take a quick shower and start fretting over those files again." Connor laughed. "Am I right?"

"Probably," she admitted.

But at the moment that flash drive was the last thing Brooke wanted to think about. As soon as she sat down at her desk, every bit of good the day had done her would disappear. And she wasn't ready to let go of it yet.

Connor gazed into her eyes, and the space between them sparked with energy.

Was he going to try to kiss her? Did she want him to? No, she decided. Definitely not. She'd had a great time today, but that was a surefire way to toss a shock of ice water on the peace the day had brought her.

Before Brooke could break the moment, he handed her the beach bag she'd packed and took a step back. An unwelcome jab of disappointment pricked her, and she realized that deep down she had expected a kiss. In fact, she had been looking forward to it. The knowledge irritated her.

Hefting the bag on her shoulder, she jammed her key into the lock. "Good night."

"I'll call you tomorrow," Connor said, then descended the concrete stairs with a bounce in his step.

Inside the house, Brooke closed the door, twisted the dead bolt, and leaned against the door, her ear pressed to the wood. The Mustang's engine roared to life, then grew quieter as it drove down the street.

On his perch on the curtain rod, Sammy lay motionless, watching her. He narrowed his eyes slightly, and then he turned his head pointedly away.

"Don't give me that," she told the cat. "I was ready to get rid of him. And I certainly wasn't going to invite him in just to play with you."

Brooke went through the house, flipping on lights along the way, and emptied the beach bag into the laundry basket. Though Connor's suggestion of a long bath sounded appealing, she opted for a shower instead. To spite him? She thrust the thought from her mind. That was childish. She was perfectly capable of deciding how best to spend her evening.

Half an hour later, wearing comfy clothes and with her hair still damp, she took her laptop into the living room. Her favorite music hummed through the speaker of her smartphone. Sitting on the couch with her feet curled beneath her, she woke the computer and inserted the flash drive into a USB port.

The now-familiar list of files appeared on the screen. A sigh heaved from her chest. She'd studied this list so often she could recite the file names and dates in her sleep.

"This is impossible," Brooke told Sammy, who had shifted his position on the curtain rod and now sat sphinxlike, watching her from above. "There's nothing in these files that will help me figure out why Jordan wanted to make a copy and lock it up."

Still, there wasn't anything else she could do to figure out who might have killed him or why. Sitting helplessly at home while Detective Travis tried to find something to incriminate her was not an option. She had to do something.

Brooke double-clicked on the newest file, the one she was most familiar with. The document containing the team's test scripts opened. She'd written it herself, and Jordan had complimented her on coming up with a thorough assessment of the storage array's performance under stress.

She skimmed the next few pages. How often had she gone over this document? The entire team had worked on it, but testing was her specialty, and she'd written the majority of these. For instance, the one on page seventy-six, stressing the storage array's performance in regard to . . .

Her gaze snagged on a chart in the document.

She uncurled her legs and gaped at the screen. Those numbers. Snatching her phone, Brooke opened the calculator and punched in a series of numbers. Her heart thumped in her chest with a rapid beat that sent a dizzying rush of blood to her head. The numbers didn't add up.

With trembling fingers, she made a call.

"Hey," Connor said. "What's up?"

"I need you to come back here," she said in a rush. "I've found something."

Connor sat beside Brooke on the couch, Sammy on his lap, and tried to follow the logic of her excited chatter.

"Don't you see?" Brooke gestured at the laptop screen. "This isn't what I wrote. Test case number thirty-seven has been altered."

The words she pointed to made sense individually, but collectively they meant so much gobbledygook to him. "Okay," he said, drawing out the word. "Don't forget that I'm not a programmer. You're going to have to explain it in English."

A long, slow breath later, she tried again. "Tell me about this couch we're sitting on."

Connor made a show of inspecting the empty cushion between them. "It's a nice couch." He bounced. "Soft and comfortable."

"Right. Now get up." Brooke hopped off the sofa, laptop in hand, and gestured for him to join her facing the couch. "Check it out from this angle. Do you notice anything?"

He stood beside her and examined the completely normal-looking couch. What was he supposed to notice? "It's covered in some sort of soft material with tiny yellow spots. Three seat cushions and the same number along the back."

She motioned to the place where she'd just been sitting. "Do you see how that cushion has more wear than the others?"

Now that she pointed it out, Connor did see. "It's more compressed."

"Yes, that's because this cushion gets sat on more than the others. It's where I sit most of the time. Now imagine this couch is a data storage array. Some parts of it get accessed more than others."

"I get it. Those parts wear down faster."

"Exactly. Those places are called hot spots. One of the things we need to test is how the storage array holds up when those hot spots are stressed. We apply that stress in increasingly random patterns. But look here." Brooke dropped back onto the cushion and patted the place next to her.

He sat down again.

She drew his attention to the laptop monitor. "This chart is a hot spot emulation test. It's like if we asked a bunch of people to jump up and down on the sofa in random patterns."

A chuckle rumbled in his chest at the picture she painted. "You have more people jump on that end, right?"

That elicited a grin. "Right. Only here's the thing. We know the weight and stress limit the couch can endure without breaking. Just like we know how much stress the storage array can take before it breaks.

For this test we were testing at 100 percent capacity. That should not have broken the array, but it did. And here's why. These percentages add up to 125 percent, not 100 percent."

A light bulb went off, and Connor finally saw what she meant. "Someone purposefully used more dynamite than they were supposed to so they could blow up your system."

Brooke chuckled. "That's kind of switching metaphors, but yeah, that's the idea." She opened another window on the screen. "Here's the same file of test cases, only this one is dated last month. Check it out."

He did a quick comparison of the two charts. The numbers were similar enough not to call attention to any particular one, but they were definitely different. "Here's the million-dollar question," he said. "Who has access to this file?"

A frown creased her features. "That's the problem. All of us. But it was primarily the responsibility of two people." She caught his gaze and held it. "Me and Derek."

The impact of her statement struck him like a blow. "The guy who was here today."

Brooke began to pace the perimeter of the living room. "After the test failed, Jordan assigned Derek and me the task of combing through those test cases to see if we could spot anything awry. I e-mailed myself a copy of the document so I could work at home. The numbers were fine in the file I checked that night. They wouldn't have blown the system. But they didn't add up in that one, which was dated the day before. The file on that flash drive was the one used during our test."

Ticking off the days in his mind, Connor followed her logic. "Someone changed the file back to normal after the test but before you e-mailed the document to yourself."

"So what was Derek after when he came to 'check on me' today?" The pacing resumed. "I was supposed to e-mail him my findings that night, but I didn't. Maybe he paid me a visit to feel me out, to see if I'd noticed the inflated numbers."

"Or maybe he wasn't planning to ask. If he was the one who altered the file, maybe he was here to make sure you couldn't tell anyone anything." He grew serious. "Like, ever again."

Brooke stared at him. "If you hadn't arrived when you did . . ."

The impact of the statement lay heavy between them.

Connor left the couch and crossed the room to stand in front of her. "It's time to turn that flash drive over to Detective Travis."

"First thing tomorrow," she agreed. Then, with a trembling jaw, she asked, "Would you go with me? I'd rather not face him alone."

An impulse took hold of him, one he struggled to fight off. He wanted to take her in his arms and protect her from everything. But somehow he knew she wouldn't appreciate that. He was making progress toward convincing her that he was trustworthy, but he still had a long way to go.

Instead, he nodded. "I'll pick you up at nine o'clock."

The ring of her cell phone woke Brooke from a deep sleep on Thursday morning. Red glowing numbers from the clock on her nightstand informed her the time was 5:47.

"No," she groaned and pulled a pillow over her head. She hadn't gotten a decent night's sleep since the disastrous test at work that had kicked off the worst week of her life.

Her mind skipped from the failed test, the flash drive, the altered percentages, and her pending meeting with Detective Travis. She finally reached for the phone. It was Holly.

"Did I wake you?" Holly asked.

It took a moment for her thoughts to clear. Brooke had planned to call Holly this morning before Connor arrived to take her to Travis's office. But she certainly wouldn't have called before six in the morning. She sat up and propped a pillow behind her. "No," she lied.

"Oh, good." Relief saturated Holly's voice but disappeared with the next tense words. "I couldn't sleep, so I decided to catch up on some things I've been putting off since Jordan—since last week. Pay some bills, check my e-mail, stuff like that."

Brooke rested the phone on her shoulder and rubbed sleep from her eyes. "That must be hard."

"I got an e-mail yesterday," Holly continued. "It was one of those alerts telling me an unknown device had accessed our cell phone account."

Brooke froze. "Did Jordan have user IDs and passwords recorded in his office somewhere the robber could have found them?"

"That's what I'm wondering," Holly said. "Or maybe on his laptop. Anyway, I checked the account, and there haven't been any odd phone calls or unexplained charges."

"That's good," Brooke told her, but they both knew nothing about this whole mess could be called good.

"I guess," Holly said, uncertainty saturating her tone. "I feel so lost. Like I can't make even a simple decision. Jordan would know exactly what to do, but I'm in some kind of fog."

The widow was most likely suffering from a combination of shock and grief. "That's totally understandable," Brooke said gently.

"I know I'm asking a lot, and we barely even know each other," Holly said. "But Jordan spoke so highly of you that I thought maybe you could shed some light on this. What do you think I should do?"

A break-in, the hidden flash drive, her phone account being hacked, not to mention her husband being murdered. There was only one piece of advice Brooke could give this grieving woman. "You have to call the police and tell them everything."

"That's what I thought too." Her voice sounded lighter. "Thank you."

When the call ended, Brooke's fingers hovered over the cell phone. She wanted to update Connor, but waking him up before dawn implied a deeper relationship than they had.

She decided on a text. *Come over when you wake up. There's been a development.*

At ten minutes before eight, an insistent knocking sounded on her front door.

Brooke was not surprised to find Detective Travis standing on the porch. The man was neatly dressed in slacks and a polo shirt, but his jawline displayed a day's worth of graying stubble. Apparently Holly had woken him up as well, and he hadn't taken time to shave.

Travis shook a finger at her. "I should arrest you for obstruction. Withholding evidence in a murder investigation is a criminal act."

Brooke adopted a contrite expression. "I'm sorry. But Holly asked me to—"

"I don't care what she asked you to do." Anger vibrated in his voice. "You're an intelligent woman. You should know better."

She hung her head. He was absolutely right. In the past two hours she'd imagined this encounter, and in retrospect, she realized she should have made a copy of the flash drive immediately and then given it to the police. Actually, she should have told Holly to hand them the receipt and combination and let Travis locate the locker himself.

But then she wouldn't have made her startling discovery.

He held his hand out. "May I have that drive now?"

"Yes, but please come inside." Brooke opened the door wider. "I have something to show you."

The detective brushed past her.

She started to close the door but halted when a flash of red caught her eye. Connor's Mustang turning onto her street. Relieved, she watched the car navigate down the road and pull into her driveway.

Connor got out and headed to the front door. He glanced at the detective's unmarked car parked on the street, then peered inquisitively at her.

She gestured for him to come inside.

An angry hiss sounded from the curtain rod above the front window.

Brooke whirled around to find Sammy hissing at Travis.

"What's wrong with your cat?" the detective snapped.

For a second, she considered closing the feline in the bathroom again, but she decided against it. Detective Travis was on his own against Sammy. "He doesn't like men," she said.

Travis huffed. "Why does that not surprise me?"

Offended, Brooke drew herself up. "There's no need to be insulting."

Connor appeared in the doorway. When he caught sight of Travis, he gave her a quick glance. "Looks like I'm late," he said.

"We were just getting started," she told him.

Travis narrowed his eyes. "What are you doing here?"

Connor gave him a broad smile. "Moral support."

The detective stuck his hand out again. "The drive, please?"

"It's in here." Brooke led the way down the hallway to the office and seated herself at the desk. She jiggled the mouse, and the monitor came to life. "This is what I wanted to show you."

Travis took up a stance beside her, his brow furrowed, and leaned forward to read the display. "What's that supposed to be?"

Connor arrived, holding Sammy. He stopped in the doorway and scratched the cat's ears. His presence did offer her a bit of moral support.

She answered with more confidence than she'd felt a moment before. "Evidence."

"Evidence of what?" the detective asked.

"That the critical project Jordan was managing was sabotaged the day before his death."

"What do you mean?"

Brooke went on to explain, using the couch analogy and displaying the two charts that proved the numbers had been altered.

As she spoke, the hostility seeped out of Travis's features. He listened intently and without interrupting her.

"You think this is the murder motive?" the detective asked when she had finished.

"It might be," Brooke answered. "It's obvious Jordan discovered the changes and put a copy of the affected files in a safe place. It can't be a coincidence that he was killed a few short hours later."

Travis nodded. "I don't believe in coincidences, especially in murder cases." He pointed at another window on the screen. "What are all those other files?"

"They're versions of the same few files dating back a couple of years." She shrugged. "I have no idea why Jordan thought keeping older versions of these files was important."

A telephone began to ring, the sound loud in the small room.

Travis straightened and pulled his cell phone out of his pocket. He checked the screen. "I need to take this." He strode from the room, tapping on the phone as he went.

Connor stepped aside to let him pass, then approached Brooke's desk. "I came as soon as I saw your text. What's going on?"

She filled him in on Holly's discovery.

"I'm sorry I wasn't here earlier," he said. "You should have called me."

"I didn't want to wake you." Brooke grimaced. "Somebody needs to get a good night's sleep."

His gaze softened. "You can call me anytime."

A warm wave washed over her, and her cheeks began to burn. Thankfully, she was saved from answering when Detective Travis stomped into the office.

The man's forbidding scowl had returned. "That was headquarters. Mrs. Lancaster's account was accessed through a cell phone."

"Were you able to trace it?" Brooke asked.

"Our guys found it right off. A burner. Bought Tuesday night with a gift card and activated under a fake name."

His sharp tone bit through Brooke's confidence. She fought an impulse to squirm beneath his frown. She was almost afraid to ask the question at the front of her mind. "Can you find out who bought it?"

"Probably not." A cold smile appeared. "But we traced the location to the cell tower where the access originated."

Somehow she knew what he was going to say before he said it.

Travis placed his hands on the edge of her desk and leaned toward her. "It's the one closest to your house."

The fear on Brooke's face heated Connor's protective instincts to a boil. "You can't still believe Brooke is a murderer." Anger gave his voice more volume than he intended. "She's obviously being framed."

Detective Travis rounded on him. "You sound awfully sure of that. How long have you two been acquainted?"

Connor jutted his chin forward. "What difference does that make? Every bit of evidence against her is circumstantial. You know as well as I do that she's no killer."

"I know no such thing," Travis said.

She gulped, then seemed to regain a measure of confidence. "Do you think I would have told you about all of this if I was the murderer?"

The detective folded his arms across his chest. "You didn't do it voluntarily. You kept that flash drive to yourself when you should have given it to me immediately. That will sound mighty suspicious to a jury."

For a moment Connor considered tossing Sammy at the detective. An encounter with the feline might not change his attitude, but watching would give Connor a great deal of satisfaction. "We know who murdered Jordan Lancaster," he announced.

Travis whirled toward him. "What are you talking about?"

"We don't know for sure," Brooke said, nudging Connor with her elbow. "But there are only a handful of people who had access to this file and the technical knowledge to blow the test. And one of them paid me an unexpected visit yesterday."

"Which means he knows where she lives," Connor put in. "He could easily have parked on the street and hacked the Lancasters' phone account."

Though his expression didn't soften in the slightest, the detective said, "Give me a name."

Brooke glanced at Connor, asking him silent questions.

He assumed that she didn't want to rat out a coworker and subject him to the same harsh treatment she'd received from the bullying detective. But if that coworker was the killer, Travis needed to know.

"His name is Derek Ingram," she told the detective. "But as I said, several people could have altered that file."

Travis tapped the name on his phone. "Including you."

"Yes," Brooke admitted with obvious reluctance.

"Then maybe the two of you were in cahoots," Travis suggested.

Connor gave a disgusted grunt. Was this guy for real? "You're grasping at straws. Why would she set the police on an accomplice?"

The detective smirked. "Criminals always turn on each other when things get hot."

"That is so ridiculous it doesn't even deserve an answer," Connor said, rolling his eyes.

Sammy squirmed in his arms, and he realized he'd tightened his hold. He bent down and set the cat on the floor. With any luck, he'd take a swipe at Travis. "Are we finished here? Because Ms. Lester and I have things to do."

Travis scowled at Brooke. "I should take you in for more questioning."

"Unless your questions have changed, you'd be wasting your time," Brooke said calmly. "I've already told you everything I know several times."

The detective was quiet for the span of several breaths before he appeared to come to a decision. He extended a hand. "I'll take that drive now."

Brooke pulled the device out of her computer, which responded with a *ding*, and placed it in Travis's palm.

He didn't move but kept his hand extended. "Give me the rest of the evidence too."

Confusion flashed over her features for a second. Then she nodded and opened a desk drawer. She handed over the receipt, the lock, and the card containing the combination.

Holding them before him like a trophy, Travis headed for the doorway. Just before he disappeared down the hallway, he shot a cold look at Brooke. "Don't think you're off the hook. You're still our prime suspect."

When he was gone, Brooke's composure crumbled. She sank into the high-backed desk chair. Her expression was so vulnerable that it made Connor's heart twist.

"Don't worry about it," he said. "He's only trying to intimidate you."

She sighed. "For the record, it's working."

The rest of Thursday passed without incident, though Brooke found herself returning again and again to the front window to peek outside. Would Detective Travis change his mind about bringing her in for more questioning? Once she saw a police cruiser drive down her street, which set her pulse racing. But it passed by, and eventually her heart rate slowed to normal.

On Friday morning for the second day in a row Brooke was awakened abruptly, this time by someone pounding on her door at 7:20 a.m. Heart thudding against her rib cage, she sat straight up in bed. This was it. The detective was going to pick her up or maybe even arrest her for murder.

"Brooke, open up. It's important."

She heaved a relieved sigh as she recognized Connor's voice, muffled as it was. She kicked the covers off and, bundling up in her bathrobe, hurried down the hallway with Sammy padding along beside her.

"He'd better have a good reason for showing up so early," she told the cat.

No sooner had she unlocked the door than he rushed inside. He made straight for the sofa table and scooped up the television remote.

"What's going on?" she asked.

"There's been another murder." Connor aimed the remote toward the TV and pressed a button. "It's probably going to be on the news any minute."

Her throat squeezed shut. "Who?" she whispered, her voice choked. She gasped. "Not Holly." Had the murderer-slash-thief returned to the Lancaster home searching for something he missed the last time?

Connor's gaze locked onto hers, his expression somber. "Derek Ingram."

14

Brooke came into the living room holding two steaming coffee mugs. She handed one to Connor, then sat down on the sofa.

He thanked her absently, his attention on the television screen. "It's got to be on soon," he mumbled as he clicked through the channels. "It doesn't take that long to get a news crew on the scene."

The screen switched from one morning news show to another. The anchors, a man and woman, were seated beside each other behind a desk. A red banner ran across the bottom of the screen, reading, *Breaking News: Body Found in Park.*

"Here it is." Connor tossed the remote onto the empty cushion between them and sat back.

The female news anchor gazed into the camera. "We've just received a report that a body was found in a park early this morning. We have a crew on-site. Angela, what can you tell us?"

The scene switched to another woman standing outside in front of a line of yellow police tape. A gently sloping landscape and a row of trees stretched into the background. Beside her stood a twentysomething man wearing a pair of track pants and a tank top. The cord from a set of headphones dangled around his neck. Behind them, two officers stood guard on the other side of the tape, and in the distance a knot of people could be seen standing close together with their backs to the camera.

"Brad and Linda, at five o'clock this morning, a jogger came across a gruesome sight—a man's body lying beneath a bush near a running trail," Angela said. "I'm here with Dustin Baker." The newscaster held her microphone out to the man. "Please tell us what happened."

"Yeah, so I was out for a run, like I do every morning." Dustin spoke to Angela but kept glancing toward the camera. "I crossed the bridge over there." He pointed to something out of the camera's range. "It was dark and kind of hard to see. I don't know what made me look over at the brush beside the trail, but I did."

"What did you see?" Angela asked.

"At first I thought it was a pile of trash or something, and that ticked me off, because people shouldn't dump garbage in a park." Dustin ran his fingers through his thick dark hair. "But it wasn't trash. It was a guy, and he was dead. Had blood all over his shirt. I freaked out and called the cops."

Angela faced the camera again. "Mr. Baker called 911 from his cell phone. He says the police and an ambulance were here within minutes."

"Probably about ten," Dustin added with another glance at the camera.

Angela flashed him a smile and continued. "They have identified the victim as Derek Wayne Ingram, an employee at Skytech 1 Industries. As you know, last week a man was murdered at Skytech 1's corporate headquarters."

A second window appeared beside the one broadcasting Angela and the jogger. The morning show anchors came into view.

"Do the police think this murder is related to the other one?" Brad asked.

Angela shook her head. "They declined to speculate. We're trying to contact Skytech 1's executives now, so I expect we'll have more information soon."

That window disappeared, and the broadcast returned to the studio.

"Thank you, Angela," Brad said. "That was Angela Taylor on-site, where a man's body was found earlier this morning. We'll bring you more information as it becomes available." He glanced down at a tablet on the desk in front of him. "And now, let's get an update—"

Connor pressed a button on the remote control. The television screen went black.

"How did you know before it was on the news?" Brooke tried not to sound suspicious and winced when the question came out like an accusation.

Either he didn't notice or didn't take offense. "I'm a journalist," he reminded her. "I saw it on the wire at work."

She raised her eyebrows. "You were at work at five in the morning?"

"It was actually half past six," Connor said. "I'm always in the office by then. I'm an early bird."

It was a trait they shared, though Brooke didn't say so. Instead, she sipped her coffee.

"I've been thinking about something," he remarked. "Something Holly Lancaster said at the funeral."

"Oh?" she asked, peering at him over the rim of her mug.

"Holly and Jordan were supposed to go to Mexico this weekend." Connor frowned. "Why would he take a vacation now? He was swamped at work, and the most important project of his career was about to kick off."

"I wondered the same thing," Brooke said. "It would make sense if he'd planned the trip in advance. We all assumed the system test would go smoothly, so this would have been a good weekend to take off and celebrate."

"But she said Jordan surprised her with the trip that morning."

Shaking her head, she said, "It doesn't make sense. We all expected to put in long hours until we found the problem and resolved it."

Connor checked his watch. "Do you think she's up yet?"

"Probably." She got off the couch and retrieved her cell phone from the bedroom.

Holly answered on the second ring. "I hope that detective wasn't too hard on you yesterday. He was pretty mad when he left here."

"Tell me about it," Brooke said, then got to the point. "You said Jordan surprised you last Thursday morning with a weekend trip to Mexico."

A heavy sigh sounded through the phone. "He was always doing things like that. Bringing me flowers for no reason. Buying gifts for me and Aria." Holly sniffled. "I miss him so much."

"I'm so sorry," Brooke said as her heart twisted in sympathy. She paused. "I don't want to sound insensitive, but it seems like an unusual time to take a trip, since his project had experienced a major disaster the day before. Was it your anniversary or something?"

"No, and I thought so too," Holly replied. "He'd been very upset the night before. I don't think he slept at all. He didn't come to bed until really late, and he got up much earlier than I did."

Brooke glanced at Connor. "Did you ask him why he wanted to go on vacation so quickly?"

"It wasn't a vacation at first. He told me he needed to check on something for work, something in Mexico. I decided it was a good idea for him to get away, because the stress of that job was getting to him. But I wasn't comfortable with him going alone, so I suggested an escape from civilization for both of us."

"I understand," Brooke said.

"He made reservations at a hotel in Ejido Ojo de Agua." Holly gave a low laugh. "I told him a weekend on a Mexican beach sounded a lot more relaxing to me, but he insisted. He'd heard about this quaint little town and wanted to check it out. I wasn't about to turn down a weekend getaway no matter where it was."

"I don't blame you," Brooke said. "Do you know the name of the hotel?"

"I can check. I saw an e-mail with the confirmation number. Hold on. I have to pull it up on my phone."

While she waited, Brooke gave Connor a quick recap of their conversation.

Holly returned to the call. "It's called Hotel Grande. I think that's kind of a misnomer, though. The e-mail says it was only eighteen dollars a night. I can't believe Jordan would take me to a place like that."

Brooke agreed that the whole scenario was strange. They ended the call after promising to keep each other informed if they heard anything new.

No sooner had Brooke hung up than she realized she hadn't told Holly about Derek and almost called her back.

Connor, who had been tapping on the screen of his cell, caught her attention. "Ejido Ojo de Agua is about twenty miles east of Tijuana."

Thoughts of calling Holly again fled. "That's a three- or four-hour drive from here."

His trademark lopsided grin appeared. "Feel like a road trip?"

Though Brooke was ready to leave for Mexico immediately, Connor said he had some work he had to take care of first.

He cringed. "I haven't been very attentive to my job this past week."

She didn't voice her thought that at least he had a job. At this point it seemed unlikely that she would ever go back to her position at Skytech 1. Even if the company did let her return when this nightmare was over, she wasn't sure she wanted to. The place had acquired more than a few ghosts. After she cleared her name, she would start searching for a new job.

Saturday morning Brooke waited for Connor to pick her up at six o'clock. Though they planned to come home that evening, she'd thrown a change of clothes into a bag just in case.

When she peeked out the window and saw the Mustang pull into her driveway, she turned to Sammy. "You have plenty of food and water." She'd filled two giant bowls, one with water and one with dry kibble, even though he preferred canned food. Hopefully he wouldn't take retribution on her curtains. "Behave yourself," she ordered and left the house.

Connor hopped out of the driver's seat and trotted around the car to open the passenger door for her.

The gesture left her feeling slightly embarrassed. Was he always such a gentleman? This wasn't a date. They were on an investigation errand, trying to follow the trail Jordan planned to take before he died.

He slid behind the wheel and started the car's engine. "I figure we'll take highways as much as possible. It's not the most scenic route, but it's the fastest."

"We're not out for a tour of the countryside," Brooke said. "For our purpose, fastest is best."

"That's one thing I like about you," Connor said. "You have a logical approach to everything."

The sun wouldn't rise for another forty minutes or so, and Brooke was grateful for the darkness inside the car. It hid the blush that burned her cheeks. Compliments didn't sit easy with her, especially from men. She was never quite sure how to respond, so she didn't.

The faint hum of the Mustang's engine and the rumble of the tires on the road were the only sounds that broke the silence inside the car. She considered asking if they could listen to the radio, but instead she took out her cell phone and pulled up a map of their route. A blue circle representing their location moved slowly down the screen.

"You still don't trust me, do you?" Connor asked, breaking the silence.

Startled, she stared at him. The dashboard highlighted his profile in blue. "What do you mean?"

"I know I made you uncomfortable when I ran your plates and came to your house," he said. "I understand, and I'm sorry. But we've come a long way in the past week. Yet you still seem to think I'm up to something sinister."

"I don't think you're the murderer, if that's what you're implying."

"Thank goodness for that." He chuckled. "But yesterday you asked how I knew about Ingram's death before the television news reported it. It was almost as if you thought I found out by some underhanded method."

Guilt fluttered in her mind. He was right. Brooke faced forward, trying to sort through her thoughts. She had questioned how he'd obtained the information so quickly. For a little while she'd forgotten that he was a journalist and would therefore have access to breaking news before the public did. As she recalled their interactions since they'd met, she realized that he'd been nothing but honest with her. Mostly.

"I wish you'd told me about your juvenile record before Travis did," Brooke admitted. "Not that you owed me an explanation. But the way he said it did shake me up."

Connor exhaled a slow breath. "Then he accomplished what he set out to do. He put suspicion between us."

There was a lot of truth in that. "He wants to catch me off guard in hopes that I'll trip up and reveal myself as a killer." Saying the words brought back all the uncertainty and fear she'd felt during Travis's interrogations.

"I'm probably crossing a line," he said, "but I believe your suspicion goes a little deeper than my youthful carjacking episode."

Brooke felt her defenses start to rise. This sounded like a loaded topic, one she probably didn't want to broach—with Connor or even with herself. "Oh?" She inserted a chill into the word.

"I think you and Sammy have a lot in common," Connor said gently. "I think you have an inherent distrust of men. I can't help but wonder why."

She bristled. "You sound like Detective Travis. He insinuated the same thing. I told him I found the idea insulting. And I still do."

"Fair enough. Change of subject." He went on in a lighter tone. "You said you grew up in Arizona. I'll bet you were the class brain in school. Am I right?"

It would be so easy to follow the conversation trail he set out, but Brooke couldn't switch tracks that fast. His comment circled in her mind. Did she have an inherent distrust of men? If she were honest, she had to admit she did. Secretly, she applauded Sammy's aggressive attitude, maybe even wished she could emulate the feline. In a less hostile way, of course.

But Sammy trusted the man seated beside her. Though it was kind of humiliating to be schooled by a cat, maybe she should be a little less suspicious and more trusting of Connor.

"Yes, I was the class brain," Brooke said, speaking slowly and staring through the windshield at the rooftops flying past on the other side of the highway barrier. "My father took off when I was ten."

"I'm sorry," Connor said.

"Mom struggled, both financially and emotionally. I see that now. She married twice more, trying to find a man who would take care of us." She paused. "But neither of those marriages lasted."

"That had to be hard on a kid," he said in a soft voice.

Brooke gave a humorless laugh. "You have no idea. I guess I decided somewhere along the way that I wasn't going to wait for someone to come along and take care of me. I threw myself into my schoolwork and focused on getting the best education I could." She straightened in the seat. "And I was right. I'm a strong, capable woman, and I can handle my own life."

Connor grinned. "You definitely are."

"What about you?" she asked. "How come you're not back in Ohio, married with a couple of kids?"

"I had a couple of near misses in the marriage category, but I managed to escape," he joked. "Seriously, my parents have the perfect relationship, and I want the same thing. I couldn't find the right woman in Ohio."

Brooke turned away and stared out the passenger window.

Connor signaled and passed a truck. "That picture in your office. You said it was your mom and your stepfather. Number one or number two?"

"Number three," she told him. "Believe it or not, she met Bob on an online matchmaking site, and he's a nice guy. They've been married eight years. I think this one will last."

"That's great," he said. "I'm sure you're happy for her."

It was true. Brooke was happy for her mother. For the first few years of Mom's marriage, she'd expected a repeat of previous failures, but she'd finally realized that the two were devoted to each other. It sure had taken a lot of heartache, both Mom's and Brooke's, to get there.

"You've definitely proven that you can take care of yourself," Connor said. "We haven't known each other very long, but I think you're smart, strong, and entirely capable of doing anything you set out to do."

Another compliment. She fumbled for a response and finally said, "Thank you."

"I hope you won't be offended if I make one more observation."

Caution crept over Brooke. "Go on," she said hesitantly.

"Now that you've accomplished your goal of self-sufficiency, perhaps it's time to learn how to get along with a guy without being dependent on him."

The rising sun had begun to lighten the horizon and brighten the car's dark interior. Studying Connor's handsome profile, Brooke thought he might be right.

But she didn't admit it to him.

In Mexico, Connor and Brooke joined a short line of cars at the border inspection station. Along their left, a tall concrete wall topped with chain link and spiral razor wire formed an imposing barrier. Sheets of corrugated steel funneled them into a lane, and they parked in the shade beneath an overhang.

A smiling Mexican border patrol agent approached. After inspecting their passports and automobile registration, he waved them through.

Once in the country, Connor followed the route he'd mapped out to Ejido Ojo de Agua. The width of the main road dwindled as they neared their destination until they turned onto the cracked pavement that formed a two-lane road leading them into town.

He slowed the Mustang as they drove through what appeared to be the main thoroughfare, though that was a grandiose name for the narrow, neglected road. Dust swirled and blew in the hot wind. Electric poles lined both sides of the road, with dozens of wires strung between them and stretching over their heads from one side to the other. A jumble of lines descended at no discernible pattern to a series of low flat-roofed buildings dotted along the roadside. Some were little more than ramshackle sheds covered in graffiti. Others had been painted in colors that may have once been vibrant before grime and the sun worked to dull them.

The wall of a mint-green concrete structure announced in colorful hand-lettering, *Tacos de Pescado*. Through a wide window with a screen made of rusty chain link they glimpsed a pile of green fruit and yellow pineapples dangling from the sagging ceiling.

Connor grinned. "Fish taco, anyone?"

"I'll pass." Brooke shook her head as they drove by a fence made of mismatched sheets of rotting plywood. "Why would Jordan want to bring his wife here for a weekend getaway?"

"I don't know." Connor cocked his head, considering. "Holly said he described the place as quaint, but I'm guessing he'd never actually been here. He probably figured it was a small town not far from Tijuana, an easy drive but out of the way of the crush of tourists. I'm sure he didn't expect this." He waved a hand at the scenery outside the car.

Finally, they reached their destination—Hotel Grande. Beside it, an empty area consisting of grayish dirt and gravel served as a parking lot and provided a space between the hotel and what could only be a junkyard, jammed full of wrecked cars covered in inches of dirt.

Connor pulled into the lot and parked beside a pickup that might have been white beneath a layer of dirt and mud. "Welcome to Hotel Grande," he said, leaning forward to peer through the windshield.

A pair of towering palm trees stood guard on either side of the entrance to a two-story stucco structure. Compared to the town they'd driven through to reach it, the Hotel Grande seemed like a manor house.

A set of stairs on the side of the building led to the upper floor, where a spindly railing lined a narrow walkway with four red doors, presumably hotel rooms. Some care had been taken to give the place a clean, tidy appearance. The whitewash looked, if not fresh, at least not encrusted with dirt. White bars lined every window, which offered an impression of security, and a concrete fence surrounded the building. While graffiti covered the side facing the street, the inside—which Connor glimpsed through a gate—appeared clean and also whitewashed. Adobe pots with blooming red flowers lined the walkway leading to the front door. There was no sign, but *Hotel Grande* was painted in neat letters above the door.

Brooke wore a cautious expression. "It's fairly clean, at least compared to the rest of the town."

"It is kind of charming," Connor said. "I'll bet Jordan saw a picture of this hotel and assumed the whole town matched. He probably thought he and Holly would find local markets to shop in or charming little restaurants."

"Maybe," she agreed. "Can you tell what that says?" She pointed to the small letters beneath the name of the hotel.

"If I remember my high school Spanish right, I think they're advertising good food for cheap," he said. "Think we should check it out?"

Brooke pursed her lips. "It's as good a place to start as any. But if I were you, I wouldn't drink the water."

"Good advice."

Before they'd exited the car, the hotel door opened, and a short, round Hispanic woman appeared. Black hair coiled around her head like a crown. She smiled and waved at them.

"The welcoming committee has spotted us," Brooke said.

Connor opened his door and stepped into the oppressive heat. Brooke joined him at the front of the car, and together they approached the woman.

"*Hola, amigos.* You're American, *sí*?"

"Yes, we're American," Connor answered. He whispered to Brooke, "Do you speak Spanish?"

"Not a word," she replied in a low voice. "I took French."

"No *problema*," the woman said. "I speak English. Americans come through here sometimes." She continued to smile. "I am Consuela Molina. Will you stay the night? I have a nice room for you."

"No," he hurried to say. "We aren't staying. But can we get something to eat?"

Consuela frowned.

Connor gestured to the lettering above the door. "*Comida?*"

Consuela's smile widened, and she looped an arm through each of theirs. "Come in. I have fresh eggs." She guided them inside.

They entered a spacious room with several wooden tables, obviously the hotel's restaurant. Each table was set for four diners, with paper place mats, napkins, and silverware. The stucco walls were alive with murals of tropical trees and colorful birds perched in their branches. Through a serving window in the wall he glimpsed the kitchen. Paddle fans spun at a lazy speed from the ceiling, attempting to circulate the hot air. Every chair in the room stood empty, which wasn't surprising. From what they'd seen of Ejido Ojo de Agua, there wasn't much to attract a thriving tourist trade.

Their hostess seated them at a table by an open back window.

He peered out the window and glimpsed a small but attractive garden with a surprising number of blooming flowers in a riot of colors. "You must have a green thumb," he commented.

Consuela tilted her head, a question etched in the lines on her brow.

"It's pretty," Connor said, motioning to the garden. "Uh, *muy bonita.*"

The woman's smile reappeared. "*Gracias.* You want a drink? I have soda."

"That sounds good," Brooke said.

Connor agreed.

Consuela bustled through a curtain in a doorway behind him. She returned in a moment with two cans of soda, which she set before them along with ice-filled glasses.

"We're visitors," Brooke said. "Can you tell us about Ejido Ojo de Agua?"

Again, Consuela's expression went blank. She shook her head.

"We're tourists," Connor explained. He dredged up a word from high school Spanish class. "*Turistas.*"

"Ah." Consuela nodded, then turned away and disappeared through the curtain again.

He caught Brooke's gaze across the table and arched his eyebrows. "I don't think she realized we had a question."

"It's going to be hard to find out anything here," she whispered. "We can't communicate with her well enough."

"We'll have to explore the town. See if anything jumps out at us." Connor popped the top of his can and started to pour the soda over the ice, then hesitated. "What are the chances they make ice from bottled water?"

"I don't know, but I'd rather not risk it." Brooke pushed her glass away, opened her soda, and drank directly from the can.

He did the same. The drink was cool but definitely warmer than he preferred. Still, he'd heard too many stories of Americans getting sick from bacteria in water from other countries.

The curtain parted, and a man appeared. He was only slightly taller than Consuela and at least twice as heavy. Gleaming black hair covered his round head, and the sunlight streaming through the window glinted off a gold earring in his left ear.

"*Buenos días,*" he said when he approached the table. "I am Pedro Molina." He spread his arms wide to take in the room. "My wife told me we had guests. Welcome." Though his accent was strong, he spoke English confidently without hesitation.

Connor stood to shake the man's hand. "Connor Dyson. Nice to meet you. And this is Brooke Lester." He'd almost introduced her as his friend, and after their personal conversation during the drive here, he was a little more convinced that they could be friends, maybe even more. But he still wasn't sure how she felt, so he'd kept it simple.

"*Encantado.*" The man executed a brief bow to Brooke. "You are American tourists?"

"That's right," Brooke said. "We're in town for the day."

He shook his head. "Why do you want to spend your time here when there are so many exciting and beautiful places to visit in Mexico?"

"A friend mentioned Ejido Ojo de Agua," Connor said, "so we thought we'd check it out."

Pedro threw back his head and laughed. "Are you sure he is a friend? I would send my friend to Tijuana or Puerto Nuevo, not to a dirty little town like this one."

"But you live here," Brooke said, her tone bewildered.

"A matter of necessity," he said. "It is home."

"There's nothing to see?" Connor asked. "No place in town for us to visit?"

"You could visit our local churches," Pedro replied. "They are lovely."

Somehow Connor didn't think Lancaster would have come all the way down here to tour local churches. "There's got to be something else here. What do the residents do for a living?"

Pedro grew serious. "Whatever they can. Many ride the bus to work in bigger towns. Some make clothes or dolls or carvings to sell in the tourist markets in Tijuana or Ensenada. A few lucky ones work in construction. We are poor people."

"Forgive me for asking," Brooke said, "but if no one comes here, how does your business survive?"

He bent toward her and spoke in a loud whisper, with a conspiratorial wink. "I married a rich woman. My Consuela is from Mexico City, and her father owns a large cement company there. He heard of a big factory that would be built a couple of miles east of town, one with American investors. He is a smart businessman and thinks this is a good place for a nice hotel and restaurant." He slapped a hand to his chest. "And he knows who could run it."

Connor's ears perked up. "A factory?"

Pedro nodded. "It is good for the people here. Already men were hired to build the building. And when it is finished, a factory needs workers."

"What will they make?" Brooke asked.

"Something with computers." Pedro waved a hand in the air. "Everything is computers these days. Even me. I have a website for my hotel." His chest swelled with self-importance.

Connor glanced at Brooke. A computer company near an economically depressed town? American corporations were known for shipping manufacturing jobs to countries where they could pay far less in wages than to unionized workers in the States. Was this factory the reason behind Jordan Lancaster's surprise weekend getaway to Mexico?

"Any idea when the factory will open?" he asked.

"Soon," Pedro said. "The building is almost finished."

The curtain parted, and Consuela appeared with two steaming plates. She slid them onto the table and then stood back, an anxious crease between her brows.

Connor admired his plate that nearly overflowed with refried beans and fresh salsa piled high on corn tortillas and topped with three fried eggs over easy.

"It smells amazing," Brooke said with a smile.

"My thoughts exactly," Connor added.

"Try it," Pedro urged. "My Consuela is the best cook in all of Mexico."

Connor picked up his fork and cut a generous bite. The salsa was warm, with just the right spice, the eggs perfectly cooked. He chewed with relish.

Consuela folded her hands beneath her chin. "Good?"

"This is delicious, Senora Molina," Connor said.

Brooke closed her eyes. "I'll never eat salsa from a jar again."

Pride shone on Consuela's features. "Gracias."

Her husband waved a hand dismissively in the air. "Call us by our names. I am Pedro, and she is Consuela. We are friends now, sí?"

Connor grinned at the man. "Sí, amigos."

Brooke insisted on paying the bill. Connor tried to argue with her, but she refused to give in. He'd paid for the fuel to drive down here, and she insisted that it was right for her to contribute to the venture. While he questioned Pedro about the location of the factory, she tucked a generous tip beneath her place mat so Consuela would find it after they were gone.

Waving goodbye to the friendly couple, they climbed into the Mustang and pulled out of the parking lot.

As the hotel owner had said, the factory was located a couple of miles east of town. Brooke examined the landscape they passed, which consisted of a lot of dirt, a few stray patches of scraggly grass, and an enormous variety of sun-scorched cacti. They had no trouble locating the factory. It was the only building within miles.

Connor pulled through an opening in a ten-foot chain link fence topped with razor wire and parked beside a collection of older automobiles. The common color seemed to be rust.

The factory building wasn't large by American standards. Brooke judged it to be roughly a quarter of the size of Skytech 1's manufacturing plant. It was a long concrete building with slitted windows spaced evenly all the way around. A cluster of men worked on the flat roof, and double glass doors that served as the entrance stood open.

Connor pulled out his cell phone and started snapping pictures. "See the sign there?"

She noticed a large sign hanging above the entrance. "'*Tecnología del Cielo*,'" she read, probably butchering the pronunciation. "Must be the name of the company." Beneath it were more sentences in smaller text, which she couldn't begin to understand. "*Tecnología* is technology, right?"

"Yes, but I don't know what *cielo* means." He took a photo of the sign. "We can find out later."

They got out of the Mustang and made their way between the cars toward the open doors. From inside came the sound of hammering and muffled voices speaking in Spanish. The outside of the building seemed finished, but apparently the interior work was ongoing.

They stepped into a small room that was about half the size of the Molinas' restaurant. It had concrete floors and unpainted walls. The noise of the workers came through an open doorway directly ahead of them.

"Reception area," Brooke whispered, though why she felt the need to lower her voice she didn't know. Except they weren't sure what they were seeing or what they might find.

A man appeared in the open doorway balancing a ladder on his shoulder. He wore a filthy wrinkled T-shirt and baggy jeans with frayed hems. A tool belt slung low on his hips identified him as a construction worker. He stared at them.

"Hola," Connor called in a friendly voice.

Instead of answering, the man shouted in rapid Spanish over his shoulder and continued on his way.

Brooke threw a questioning glance at Connor, who shrugged.

A few seconds later, a second man appeared. His clothes were free of stains and tears, and he wasn't wearing a tool belt. A deep frown carved creases in his face as he said something to them in Spanish.

Brooke battled an instinct to back away. She didn't understand what he was saying, but she guessed he wanted to know who they were and what they were doing inside the building.

"Excuse me," Connor said, giving the man a pleasant smile. "*Habla inglés?*"

The man shouted for someone behind him as he continued to watch them.

A moment later, a second man appeared. The two exchanged a few words.

"You are on private property, amigo." Though the second man used the Spanish word for *friend*, his countenance was no less hostile than the first. "No one is permitted here."

Connor splayed his hands in a nonthreatening gesture. "Sorry, but we didn't know. We're American tourists, and we heard this company has ties to the United States. We just wanted to see it for ourselves."

He folded strong arms across his chest. "What you heard is not true."

Brooke made no claim to being an expert on body language, but everything in this man's stance shouted, "Get out of here, and make it quick." She put a hand on Connor's arm. "Obviously we're mistaken. We should leave."

Connor's pleasant expression didn't fade. "Forgive us for the intrusion," he told the men. "Have a good day. *Un día bueno.*"

They left, and Brooke felt the weight of burning gazes on her back until Connor opened the door for her. She jumped into the Mustang and looked over her shoulder. The first man was nowhere in sight, but the second one stood in the doorway, his arms still folded, watching them.

Connor slid into the driver's seat. "What was that all about?"

"I don't know, but it was intense. I was afraid they were going to call the police on us for trespassing." She glanced at the doorway again. The man had not moved. "Let's get out of here."

He started the engine and steered the car around the tall fence. The spiraled razor wire on top felt more intimidating after the hostile encounter.

Once the factory fell out of sight behind them, Connor pulled off the road.

"What are you doing?" Brooke asked.

"I want to translate the name of that company." He tapped on the screen of his cell phone. A moment later, he shook his head.

"What?" she asked.

"*Cielo* means *sky* in English. The company's name is Technology of the Sky."

The impact of his words struck her like a slap, and she gasped.

At the same time, they said in unison, "Skytech 1."

Clouds covered the moon that night. If Brooke had been the type to believe in signs, she might have considered the dense darkness a good omen, hiding their activities. But she wasn't superstitious, and no matter how hard Connor tried to convince her that their plan would turn out fine, she couldn't shake the feeling that they were making a huge mistake, one they would regret.

"I can't believe I let you talk me into this," she hissed. Her voice seemed to stir the bushy stand of cacti behind which he'd parked the Mustang.

"We'll be fine," Connor said as he rummaged around in a toolbox in the trunk. He shoved a couple of tools into his back pockets, then grabbed a car jack handle and the newly purchased bolt cutters.

"You keep saying that," she responded. "What will the Mexican police do to us if they catch us breaking into a construction site?"

He slammed the trunk. "We won't get caught. We're just going to take a quick look in that building."

"What if it's guarded?"

"Why would they guard a construction site? It's not a functional factory yet."

"That man today might have told somebody about us," Brooke said. "They're probably watching for us right now, with machine guns and hand grenades and machetes or something." Her knees trembled at the idea of a group of armed men lying in wait for the foolish would-be raiders.

Connor's white teeth appeared, and a low laugh rumbled from his chest. "Would you listen to yourself? Don't be so paranoid. Where's your sense of curiosity?"

"I'm a systems programmer," she said. "We're known for logic, not curiosity."

"And I'm a journalist," he countered. "Curiosity is a critical part of my job."

She ignored him. "I'm also a law-abiding citizen."

"One who is under suspicion for a murder she didn't commit. That's why we're here, remember?" Connor pointed in the direction of the building that was hidden behind a swell in the land. "That factory is why your boss planned to come to this little town. Something in there might help us figure out why two men have been killed."

"Or it might get us killed," Brooke said.

Something scurried in the dark nearby, a slithering sound of moving dirt and gravel.

She jumped forward and clutched his arm, shivering. "What was that?"

"It's nothing. Probably just a lizard." He placed a hand over hers and spoke in a soothing tone. "You don't have to go. In fact, you shouldn't go. Get back in the car and wait for me. I'll slip over there, find a way inside, and snap some pictures. I'll be back in thirty minutes, and we'll blow this joint."

The idea tempted her. Standing this close to him, his features were visible, especially the eyes that fixed on hers. His arm felt warm, his muscles strong beneath the long-sleeved shirt. Why was he here anyway? Yes, he hoped to get the scoop on a news story, but deep down she knew there was another reason, one that had to do with their conversation during the long drive to Mexico. Beneath his observation that she needed to learn to trust in someone other than herself was an unspoken suggestion. If she was reading his signals right, he wanted to be the person she trusted.

"No," Brooke said firmly, "we're doing this together."

He pressed her hands. "If we see any cars in the parking lot or any sign that someone's inside, we'll leave."

A hint of relief swept through her, and she nodded.

Connor took her hand and held on to it as he led her away from the car, weaving through the scrub brush and rocks that dotted the ground.

Taking comfort from the strong fingers wrapped around hers, Brooke matched his pace, straining her vision for a glimpse of their goal. Dry brambles grabbed at her dark jeans, purchased along with black shirts and caps in Tijuana, where they'd spent long hours waiting for nightfall.

They'd traveled half a mile or so when the factory came into view. Spotlights mounted on the roof illuminated the ground at the four corners of the building, but none shone from inside. At least not from their angle of approach.

They stopped a few feet outside the fence and stared through the chain link. From this vantage point, they could see two sides of the rectangular building and the surrounding area, including the parking lot. Not a single vehicle was in view.

"Looks deserted," she whispered, still clinging to his hand.

"Let's make sure."

They followed the fence until the opposite side of the building came into view. They hadn't seen this side earlier in the day. Four truck bays were evenly spaced, the overhead doors all shut, and the place appeared as deserted as the rest of the area.

"The loading dock," Brooke said.

"This is as good a place as any." He released her hand and gave her the jack handle, then approached the fence with the bolt cutters they'd bought at a store outside Tijuana.

She scanned the area around the building for any sign of movement while he worked.

"This is much harder than I thought," Connor muttered. "We should have gotten the heavy-duty ones." He grabbed the small tool with both hands.

When the metal snapped, it sounded like a series of explosions in the silent night.

Though the heat of the blazing sun had given way to a crisp nighttime chill, sweat trickled down her spine.

In minutes that seemed to last hours, he bent back a newly cut section of the fence. "Ladies first."

Brooke dropped to her knees and crawled through, then stood and dusted off her jeans.

Connor followed. "Piece of cake," he said, pocketing the cutters.

They slunk toward the building and arrived beneath the row of narrow windows they'd seen on the front of the building. Each was protected with white metal bars, and the glass on the other side of the bars was frosted, making it impossible to see inside.

He grabbed a bar and tried to shake it, but it held firm. "It would take a blowtorch to get through these."

"And more time than we have," she said.

They circled around to the loading dock and approached the first truck bay. The overhead door was made of sturdy metal.

"There's no way inside," Brooke announced.

Connor scanned the area. "Maybe there is." He pointed toward a recessed window between the two bays.

She studied the window. A wooden shelf extended outward beneath the opening. The window was covered with a miniature version of the larger overhead bay doors, and it had no bars. It was probably some sort of check-in station for shipping and receiving.

Connor extended a hand toward her, and she realized she still held the jack handle. She gave it to him and watched as he pulled a screwdriver out of his pocket, inserted it between the metal door and the wooden shelf, and used the handle as a lever. The sounds of his labor were loud enough to make her cringe.

Finally, he grinned at her. "Never underestimate the skills of a former juvenile delinquent." Then he lifted the door over the window. The metal sheet opened upward on rollers like a garage door.

Drawing near, Brooke peeked inside. The darkness within was nearly complete. "I can't see a thing."

He cupped his hands low and held them toward her. "I'll give you a leg up."

Were they really going through with this? Silent alarms rang in her mind. They'd done the breaking part, and now they were getting ready to do the entering. There was still time to turn around and leave.

But then they'd never know what was so important about this factory. They'd never know why Jordan and Derek had been murdered.

Brooke put her foot in his hands, hopped upward, and climbed through the open window.

The shelf was wide, and she twisted on her belly so she could drop to her feet on the other side. The rubber soles of her sneakers made no sound when she landed on the concrete floor.

A moment later, Connor stood beside her, and together they regarded their surroundings.

The light outside had been dim, but enough filtered through the newly opened window to reveal that they stood in a small, unfurnished room. Large openings—likely for doors—had been cut in the walls on either side in the direction of the nearest truck bays, but the darkness in that area was too complete to see anything. Openings in the interior walls had been framed as windows, but glass had yet to be installed. The smell of fresh-cut lumber permeated the room.

"This is probably going to be an inventory clerk's office," Connor said in a quiet voice, "where materials are logged as they come in and go out."

A door-shaped opening in the back wall led farther into the building. They stepped through it and entered a cavernous room that was most likely the main production part of the factory. Dim light illuminated the frosted glass in the narrow windows in the exterior walls, but it didn't penetrate far enough to reveal anything in the room.

"I can't see a thing," Brooke whispered. Her voice sounded hollow, as if spoken in a cavern.

"Maybe this will help," he said.

A light flared, and she realized Connor was holding his cell phone. Following his lead, she grabbed her phone from her pocket and switched on the flashlight feature.

They shone the beams in the same direction and saw a long, flat object directly in front of them. But the lights weren't strong enough to penetrate more than a couple of feet.

A flash in the distance caught her eye. It reminded her of a sliver of light that would shine through the bottom of a closed door when someone on the other side flipped on a lamp. She grabbed Connor's arm, but he'd seen it too.

"Flashlights," he whispered, turning his off.

She did the same with trembling fingers.

The door opened to reveal the silhouette of a man. He shouted something in Spanish, and his voice echoed in the large room.

Connor dropped to a crouch and pulled Brooke with him.

Her heart seemed to have lodged in her throat.

The man yelled something else. He sounded angry.

Lights flashed on. Industrial-strength LED lights installed in tracks all along the ceiling illuminated the factory with horrible clarity.

Their surroundings suddenly apparent, Brooke realized they were crouching beside a waist-high conveyor belt. Scattered around the length of the belt were pieces of equipment, some still in boxes, none functional. And none near enough to hide behind.

They were in the open, completely visible.

The man in the doorway spotted them and ran toward them doing two things at once: shouting over his shoulder—probably calling for help—and pulling a pistol from his belt. He stopped a few yards away, planted his feet, and grasped the gun in both hands, the barrel pointed at Brooke and Connor. He continued to shout, the words unintelligible but their meaning obvious.

"I think he wants us to put our hands up," Connor said, straightening with his arms stretched high above his head.

Another man ran into the room, speaking rapidly into a cell phone that he held in one hand and clutching a pistol in the other. He arrived at his partner's side as his call ended, said something in Spanish, and pointed his gun at them as well.

For the first time in her life, Brooke knew what it was like to stare down the barrel of a gun. The experience was far more terrifying than she could have imagined.

The first guard made a swinging gesture toward the front of the building with the pistol.

"He wants us to go that way." Connor gestured in the direction the man pointed.

Together Connor and Brooke obeyed, followed at a short distance by the men with the guns.

Connor cringed when he glanced at Brooke. Her face had gone completely white. That could have been a result of the glaring lights, or it could have been fear. Judging by the shaking hands above her head, he assumed the latter. Guilt slashed at him. The feeling hit him so intensely that he nearly stumbled. What had he done? He'd been so confident throughout the day that they could get inside this building, explore the place, and casually saunter out.

And where had these guys come from? There were no cars in the parking lot. The answer became clear a short time later when they passed the last loading dock bay and saw two motorcycles parked inside the closed door. Connor could have kicked himself. If these two were guarding the building alone, of course they wouldn't leave their motorcycles outside to be stolen during the night. He should have listened to Brooke. Instead, he'd dragged her into a situation that might get her killed.

Were there only two guards? If there were more, surely they would have appeared to confront the intruders. Maybe he could overpower these two.

With one backward glance, Connor gave up on that idea. He might be able to take one down if he could surprise him, but no way could he disable both.

They arrived at the front end of the plant and stepped through the doorway where the men had appeared. On the other side they entered a short hallway with two doors on either side, probably some sort of office.

Guard number one barked a single word that Connor didn't know, but the meaning was unmistakable.

Connor and Brooke stopped.

The guard waved toward one of the doors with the gun.

Connor tried the handle, and it gave under his hand. He pushed the door open and moved back for Brooke to enter first. If he was going to attempt to overpower their captors, now was the time, within the close confines of the hallway. But the menace of those pistols weakened his resolve, and he followed her inside.

The door slammed behind them, and they were thrown into darkness.

Brooke pulled her cell phone out of her pocket and switched on the flashlight. They'd been confined in a narrow room with a low ceiling. There were no furnishings or windows. The air quickly grew stuffy and uncomfortably warm. "It's a storage closet."

"I thought it might be an office." Connor stretched his arms wide. His fingers touched both walls.

"Office conditions in Mexico might not be the same as in the States, but I doubt they'd close anyone in a room this tiny all day long." She gulped against a dry throat. "It looks like a prison cell."

Connor made no comment. Instead, he flipped a light switch beside the door. Nothing. From the ceiling a light fixture dangled but without a bulb. He paced the perimeter of the room, his hands sliding along the walls. When he'd gone full circle, his expression was somber in the glow of her flashlight. "I was hoping there would be a crack in the drywall or something we could break through without too much noise, but it's solid."

Her muscles, rigid from a panic more forceful than anything she'd ever felt, threatened to give out on her, so she slid down a wall to the floor. The room was just wide enough for Connor to sit opposite her, their folded knees touching. She set the cell phone on the floor beside them.

"I'm sorry." His shoulders sagged. "I should have listened to you. We haven't learned anything, and now . . ."

Though her whirling thoughts could easily supply several gruesome endings to his unfinished sentence, Brooke shook her head. "That's not true. We have learned something. Something important."

Connor raised his head. "We have?"

"I saw the layout of this facility right before they nabbed us. I had one of those déjà vu moments, you know? Like I've been here before, walking by a conveyor belt similar to the one out there, with all the equipment piled in boxes, ready to hook up. Then I realized I have seen this layout before."

Interest flared on his features. "At Skytech 1?"

"Yes, in a dedicated room inside the manufacturing plant, where we set up the equipment to create a prototype of the ten-drive stripe storage array."

"Do you mean this place is a duplicate?"

"Exactly. And not only that." Excitement, fed by panic, danced along her nerve endings. "Remember the computer-aided design files on the flash drive?"

Realization lit his features. "The blueprints. Those files contain all the details of how to build this manufacturing facility."

Muffled sounds came from beyond the doorway, voices firing unintelligible words at one another.

Her heart erupted into a staccato beat that threatened to crack her ribs from the inside.

"Quick!" Connor pointed at her phone. "Flip that off, and put it in your shoe."

In the instant before she tapped the screen and plunged the room once again into darkness, she saw him untying his own tennis shoe. To put something in it? The sound of a tense conversation in Spanish drew near as she finished tying her laces and slid up the wall to a standing position. She felt Connor do the same.

The door opened, and she was blinded by the beam of a bright flashlight. A growling voice, heavily accented, bellowed an order in Spanish. Rough hands grabbed her arm and jerked her forward. She emerged into the hallway.

"Hey, watch it!" Connor shouted. He yanked his arm out of his captor's clutch, which earned him a vicious shove. He flew forward and bounced off the opposite wall with a thud.

Three new men had joined the first two, and they all crowded into the hallway. The one who'd given the order fixed her with a menacing glare, and she couldn't stop an involuntary shudder. Pockmarks, probably from adolescent acne, covered his cheeks. Unlike his companions, he wore expensive-looking, well-pressed clothing, his hair combed and oiled to form a slick coif.

He snarled something else, and the man holding her arm pushed her toward an open door at the end of the hallway.

Brooke entered an office. It was furnished with a desk, a computer, and a file cabinet in the far corner. Connor was forced into the room and came to her side. She inched close to him until her arm pressed the length of his. The contact offered scant comfort, but it made her feel better regardless.

The neatly dressed man, obviously the boss, strode into the room, pulled out the desk chair, and lowered himself into it. He propped his elbows on the surface and clasped his hands. "Who are you?" he asked in a heavy accent.

The tone of his voice sent chills racing down her spine.

Connor lifted his chin. "American citizens," he said in an arrogant voice. "We want to talk to someone at the United States Embassy immediately."

Brooke gulped. How did he have the nerve to order the man around when there were four armed men standing not five feet away?

A slow smile curved their interrogator's lips. "You break into my building in the dark of night and stand before me making demands. How typical of an American." The smile faded. "You are not in America. Unless you answer my questions, you may never be there again. I repeat—who are you?"

Was he threatening to kill them? She drew a shuddering breath and pressed closer to Connor.

"We're tourists," Connor explained, a note of contrition in his voice. "We heard about a new manufacturing plant that has American backing, and we wondered about it—that's all. We came by earlier today, and the man who turned us away was so secretive that he made us more curious." He shrugged. "We just wanted to see what was inside."

Every word he spoke held the ring of truth. Brooke hoped the man believed him.

The man narrowed his eyes. "Is it your custom to cause damage and illegally enter a man's property where you live?"

"I'm a newspaper journalist," Connor replied. "We do whatever it takes to get a story, so I'm used to things like that."

"Ah, an American journalist." The man drummed his fingers on the desktop. "That makes me even more interested to know why you chose my building."

A pounding from somewhere outside the office came closer.

The man in charge jerked his head toward one of the guards, and the man left. Then he returned with two others, who marched into the room, chattering in Spanish. One of them held a bag, which he upended on the desk.

When Brooke saw the contents, her legs almost gave out beneath her. On the wooden surface lay their passports and wallets, all of which had been inside the glove compartment of the Mustang.

Their captor inspected both passports, then opened Connor's billfold. He removed the contents and spread them out before him. A driver's license, credit cards, a hundred or so American dollars along with some Mexican pesos. Selecting a laminated card, he held it up for closer inspection. "At least you are truthful about being a newspaper reporter."

Connor stiffened but said nothing.

The man swept the items aside and unzipped Brooke's wallet. Miscellaneous coins rang loudly when he dumped them on the desk. He unsnapped the other section, the one containing her cards, and began pulling them out one at a time.

Holding her driver's license up before him, his gaze switched from the card to her face. "You live in Los Angeles too, I see." He extracted another card, this one with a distinctive green logo. "And you are a coffee drinker."

Even if Brooke could have thought of a reply, she couldn't have spoken. A desert had invaded her mouth because she had remembered another card she kept in her wallet.

When he pulled out her Skytech 1 employee ID card, he froze.

As he scrutinized the card, he sucked in a loud breath through his nose and blew it out slowly. Then he turned his piercing gaze on her.

Her lungs felt paralyzed, and she couldn't look away from the intense scrutiny.

Standing, the man barked something to one of the other men, who shoved his pistol into his waistband and began to search Connor. He tossed his cell phone and screwdriver onto the desk, then proceeded to run his hands down each leg.

As he approached her, Brooke tensed. Her stomach roiled when the rough hands patted her down. She had nothing in her pockets. When he trailed down the length of her jeans, she squeezed her eyes shut. *Please don't check my shoes!*

He didn't.

Then she was jerked around and shoved toward the door. At the end of the hallway she was pushed into the same room as before. She pressed herself against the side wall in time to avoid being knocked over by Connor when he was pushed inside.

The door slammed shut, and they were plunged into darkness that somehow seemed even deeper than it had before.

Brooke's cell phone flashlight lit the closet's interior. She huddled in the back corner, arms wrapped around her knees, with one shoe on the floor in front of her.

Shadows concealed much of her face, so Connor couldn't gauge her emotional state, but at least she wasn't hysterical. In the short time he'd known her, one thing he'd come to admire was her logical approach to circumstances that would have sent many other people into fits of hysteria.

He pointed at the phone. "Can I use that?" If he could get ahold of Fitz back in LA, maybe he could do something to assist them.

"Help yourself." She extended the phone. "But I have no service in Mexico. I don't have an international plan."

Frustrated, Connor scrubbed a hand through his hair. They'd hidden the wrong phone. Stooping in front of her, he asked, "Are you doing okay?"

Brooke snorted. "Oh, I'm just peachy. Never better."

He winced. "Sorry. Dumb question."

She glanced at the door behind him. "Do you think he's calling the police?"

Connor suspected they might be better off in the hands of the police than they were now, but he didn't voice that thought. "If they were going to call the police, those first two goons would have done it as soon as they caught us. If I were to make a guess, I'd say he's calling his contact at Skytech 1."

"Things got pretty tense when he found my employee ID," Brooke said. "What do we do now?"

He scooted around and sat beside her, his back resting against the wall. "We could try to overpower whoever comes in here next, grab his gun, and make a run for it."

"And hope the other five don't shoot us in the back?" She scowled at him. "Bad idea. Got any more?"

Connor knew she was right about the disastrous probability of an attempt of force. Other ideas flitted through his mind. Could they try to talk their way out? Not likely. "I'm fresh out. You?"

"We can wait to see who shows up next and hope that person is friendlier to Americans."

It wasn't exactly a good plan. But what else could they do?

"Okay, let's think. What are our resources?" Connor slipped off his shoe and removed the bolt cutters, grateful they'd gone with the smallest model and that he had big feet. How their captors hadn't noticed his sudden limp he couldn't imagine. Could he use the cutters to pick the lock on the door? Unlikely. The screwdriver might have been a better choice. But even if he managed to open that door, there were six men on the other side that they had no chance of getting past.

Besides the bolt cutters, he'd also slipped his car key into his shoe in case they made it back to the Mustang. He desperately hoped so.

Brooke motioned to the bolt cutters. "Those would come in handy if we were in a chain link cage. In here there's nothing to cut."

He studied the empty room, then looked at the ceiling. The light fixture? He might be able to shove the cutters inside and hope he could blow a fuse or something. But they'd still be locked inside a closet with no way out.

Then Connor caught sight of something he hadn't noticed before. He jumped to his feet and examined the grate covering an air vent directly above their heads. Unlike a residential air-conditioning vent, this one was industrial size and roughly two square feet.

"Do you remember any details about the building in those blueprints?" he asked.

She followed his gaze and got to her feet. "There weren't any. Skytech 1 already has a plant. The engineers only laid out the manufacturing equipment."

"So, we don't have any way of knowing what's in the vent, but we know they don't have air-conditioning hooked up yet." The stuffy air in this enclosed space bore witness to that.

"Or they don't have it on," Brooke pointed out.

"Either way, that vent leads somewhere." Connor grabbed the bolt cutters and handed them to her. "See if you can pry it loose."

Once again he cupped his hands and held them low so she could place her foot in them. The room was so narrow she could brace one hand against the wall when he lifted her. A few seconds later, a metallic *clang* sounded. It was abnormally loud in the close confines.

"Quiet," he whispered.

"Sorry."

In the next few minutes, Connor winced at every sound. He kept a cautious eye on the doorknob while she worked, but in the dim light from her cell phone he probably couldn't have seen it turning anyway.

Then came another noise, and a shower of drywall dust fell on him.

"Got it," Brooke whispered.

When he lowered her to the floor, she held the metal grate out like a prize, grinning.

"Good job." Connor stared at the ceiling. Holding her cell phone above his head, he aimed the flashlight beam at the two-foot hole. His spirits soared. "Looks like standard AC hose. Easy to disconnect. You should be able to do it."

"Me? What about you?"

Now came the negative part of the plan. Connor took a deep breath and plunged ahead. "There's no way I can jump high enough to climb through that hole. But I can lift you up into it. When you get there, you'll be able to follow that hose to where it connects to the air conditioner, which is probably on the roof." At least he hoped so. The condenser had to be outside the building, and they hadn't seen anything like an industrial-size unit on the ground.

"What about you?" Brooke repeated. "I'm not leaving you."

"You have to," he said. "Once you're free, you can go for help."

It was a ridiculous plan, and they both knew it. There was no way Brooke could return with help before the goons outside discovered she was gone. And if she did manage to escape, where could she go? She couldn't speak the language, and it was the middle of the night. Besides, by the time she got back, they'd probably have him moved elsewhere or, more likely, shot him. He drew a fortifying breath at the thought and pasted on a confident smile he didn't feel.

Her lips compressed into a tight line. "No. Either we both go, or we both stay."

An idea flashed in his brain. Connor tilted his head and scrutinized her tall, slender build. She wasn't muscular, but she wasn't a weakling either. It might work.

"Quick," he said. "Get on the floor."

Brooke got on her hands and knees, then locked her elbows and braced her palms against the concrete floor. "I'm ready."

Connor planted a foot on her back.

She stiffened her spine and braced herself. Every muscle in her body went rigid as he stepped up, and she bore the brunt of his full weight. Her knees mashed against the floor, and she clenched her teeth as her back protested with a shaft of pain.

It lasted a short time, and then the oppressive weight disappeared. A grunt sounded above her, followed by scrabbling and shuffling. Brooke waited a second before getting to her feet, just in time to see Connor's shoes disappear into the vent. She cast an anxious glance toward the door.

Muffled voices, low enough that she couldn't have discerned the words even if she had understood them, carried through from somewhere beyond.

Overhead, there was a scuffle and a creak, and then Connor's head came into view. "You ready?" His entire torso dangled from the hole, arms extended toward her.

Brooke jumped as high as she could and grabbed his upper arms. Would Connor be able to pull her up? Muscles strained beneath her fingers, and in the next moment she was hauled upward. He pulled her forward onto a metal beam. The temperature up here was at least twenty degrees hotter than the room.

"Are you okay?" he whispered.

A mixture of fear and relief clogged her throat, but she managed to choke, "Yes."

Connor shone the cell's flashlight around. They were in a shallow attic-like space, crisscrossed with beams and a huge spiraling hose that led toward the center of the building, farther than the light's beam.

He brought his mouth close to her ear. "Follow me. Don't step off the beam, or you'll fall through the ceiling. And don't make a sound. Understand?"

They were about to walk directly over the heads of a handful of men with guns. Swallowing hard, Brooke nodded.

Holding the light in front of his feet, Connor crept forward.

She placed her foot in the center of the steel plank, which was a little wider than her shoe. Arms out at her sides, she felt like a gymnast on a balance beam. Except that if she fell off, she'd lose a lot more than a few points from the judges. She moved as quietly as she could, though if she had made a sound, she wouldn't have been able to hear it over the pounding of her heart in her ears.

Brooke had no idea how long they traveled, but they finally arrived at the end of the hose in approximately the center of the building. It joined with eight or ten others that spiraled off in different directions like the tentacles of a huge octopus.

Connor grinned at her, barely visible in the dark, and aimed the flashlight beam at the place where a large single hose rose to the roof above their heads.

She returned the grin.

Pulling the bolt cutters from his back pocket, he sliced through the material and ripped it the rest of the way. Using the tool again, he reached throught the hole and snipped through the hose on the outside of the building. The external hose came apart with a quiet rip.

Fresh air cooled her skin, and Brooke took a deep breath, savoring it.

Connor gave her an apologetic grimace. "I don't think I can jump that far."

Heaving a sigh, she dropped to her hands and knees, this time on a narrow metal beam, and once again she imitated a footstool.

When they both stood in the open air, Brooke threw her arms wide and lifted her face toward the sky. "I never thought I'd be free again."

"We aren't out of danger yet," Connor warned.

He was right. Any minute their captors would realize they had escaped. When they saw the hole in the ceiling, they'd know exactly where to find them. They had to move quickly.

"Any idea how we're going to get down from here?" she asked.

"One or two." Connor gave her a lopsided grin.

Brooke didn't realize she'd missed that smile until this moment.

She scanned the vicinity. The clouds had thinned out a bit. A handful of stars winked overhead and a partial moon shed enough light to reveal a few details on the rooftop. The exterior of the factory appeared finished from the ground level, but up here they could tell there was still plenty of work to do. Steel rods protruded from the grainy surface over half of the structure. She had no idea what they were for.

"This way." He took off at a confident stride toward the far end of the building.

At the back edge, they found a large storage bin. Connor opened the lid to reveal a collection of tools, tool belts, and other equipment. After digging inside for a few moments, he pulled out a handful of wide straps. The lopsided grin put in another appearance. "Ever been rappelling?"

"How did you know this toolbox was here?" Brooke asked.

"I didn't," he admitted. "Remember those guys we saw on the roof earlier today? Pedro told us some of the locals had been hired to work construction. I figured people as poor as those we saw in town wouldn't have their own tools. They'd use the company's tools, which means they wouldn't take them home at night. And why would they haul them down to the ground, only to bring them back up here again in the morning?"

Impressed, she gave him an admiring look. Then she sobered. "And the answer is no, I've never been rappelling."

"Neither have I," Connor said, "but we're about to learn."

The straps turned out to be sturdy, probably used to haul equipment up from the ground. Each end contained a metal hook, which he secured to one of the steel rods.

He went first, and Brooke watched anxiously from above as he descended, hand by hand, using his feet to walk down the wall. When he reached the ground, he gestured her down.

She wiped her damp palms on her jeans. In gym class at school she had never been able to get to the top of the climbing rope, but this was going down, not up. Besides, she'd faced far scarier things tonight. Like the guns of the men who would soon be hot on their trail, if they weren't already. Throwing a leg over the edge, she grabbed the strap, closed her eyes, and dropped.

For a dizzying moment, Brooke dangled, her feet pedaling in the air. The urge to shriek was strong, and she clamped her mouth shut. Then she braced the soles of her shoes against the wall as she'd seen Connor do. Her breath came in shallow gasps, and she forced herself to walk her hands down the strap. With her palms burning and arms trembling with the effort, she descended. It seemed to take hours. She prayed it would be over soon.

Brooke had no idea how far she'd come when her grasp gave way. She plummeted down, unable to hold back a scream—

—and landed in Connor's arms.

"I've got you," he whispered, and he pulled her close. "It's okay."

She clung to him, willing her breath to return, her pulse to calm. For a few seconds, she allowed herself to feel his warm breath against her cheek and his strong arms around her.

Reluctantly, Brooke stepped away and cast an anxious glance toward the front of the building. "Do you think anybody heard me?"

"Let's not wait around to find out." Connor grabbed her hand and took off at a run toward his car.

She hoped it was still there.

Connor and Brooke raced to where they'd left his Mustang. As they ran, he feared they would hear pounding feet behind them or even gunshots. Fortunately, the dark night remained silent, and no one from the factory pursued them.

When he glimpsed his car still hidden behind the stand of cacti, he wanted to fall to the ground in relief. Instead, he collapsed against it and let out a huge sigh.

"I can't believe the car's here," Brooke gasped. She bent over with her hands resting on her thighs.

"They must have been coming back to get it later." Connor was so glad to see his car that he didn't even blink when he noticed the broken window in the passenger side door. The men had obviously smashed it to get inside and steal their belongings from the glove compartment.

"Maybe they planned to get rid of us and the car at the same time," she said.

He pushed away the disturbing idea and unlocked the door for her. "We need to leave before they realize we're gone."

Brooke jumped inside and buckled her seat belt. "Ready."

He jogged around to the driver's door and slid behind the wheel. Leaving the lights off, he started the car and cautiously made his way to the road.

"What are we going to do now?" she asked.

"We need to get home as soon as possible so we can tell Travis what's going on," Connor replied.

"How do we cross the border without our passports or any other form of ID?"

"I don't know, but at least we have my car," he said. "Maybe we can explain the situation to the border guards, and they'll contact someone who will vouch for us."

"I hope so," Brooke said. She paused. "I wish we knew more about the men at the factory."

"Me too," he said. "It would be great if we could tell Travis all about them. I'll bet Pedro could give us information, but I would hate to disturb him and Consuela at this time of night."

"But it's an emergency," she reminded him. "And they were so nice to us earlier."

He nodded. "Let's go."

When they arrived at the Hotel Grande, Connor parked the car near the front entrance. They exited the vehicle and hurried to the door. It was dark inside the building, and he hoped the Molinas would hear them.

Connor pounded on the door, and the noise reverberated inside the hotel. "I hope they're as nice as we think they are," he whispered.

A light switched on inside the hotel. The curtains in the window to his left moved, and Connor stood still, letting the occupant get a good look at him. He heard the sound of a dead bolt sliding, and the door opened.

Pedro Molina peered out at them.

"We need your help," Connor said before the man could speak. "We've gotten into some trouble."

The man studied Connor, then Brooke. Finally, he opened the door wider. "Come in, amigos."

A pent-up breath Connor hadn't realized he'd been holding whooshed out of his lungs. He waved Brooke ahead of him and followed her inside. The warmth of the restaurant dining room felt heavy, almost oppressive after their exertion.

Consuela stood in the kitchen doorway wearing a robe and slippers, her hair falling loose around her shoulders. She directed a question in Spanish toward her husband, and he rattled off an answer. Fear colored her features, and she hugged herself.

Brooke took a step toward the woman, hand outstretched. "Thank you for helping us."

Consuela gave her a tight smile.

Pedro led them to the same table they'd occupied earlier. "First, you sit. Then you talk."

They collapsed into chairs.

Consuela disappeared and returned with two bottles of water. "Is clean," she said as she set the bottles before them.

The only thing on the label Connor could read was *agua*—water. He'd have to trust her that the contents wouldn't make them sick.

Apparently Brooke thought the same. She twisted off the cap and downed half her bottle in several thirsty gulps. "Thank you," she said, still panting slightly.

When Connor had taken care of his parched throat, he set the nearly empty bottle on the table.

Pedro pulled out the chair between them and sat. "Now we talk."

Connor rubbed a hand across his mouth and glanced at Brooke, who waved for him to explain. He launched into a description of their day, especially the past few hours. "We realized that there's a connection between this factory and the company where Brooke works."

"Two men have already been murdered," Brooke added.

"That is tragic," Pedro said quietly. "But what is the connection to the factory here? It's not even finished."

"That's what we're trying to figure out," Connor answered. "So we returned to the factory to look around, but we were caught by men with guns."

"What did they do?" Pedro asked.

"They locked us in a tiny room," Connor said. "They also broke into my car and stole our money, passports, and driver's licenses." He briefly described how they had escaped.

Pedro glanced across the table at Consuela, and a silent conversation passed between them. Finally, he spoke again. "We will help. I will take you to the border in Tijuana. You can walk across the bridge to America."

"We appreciate that, but we still have a car." Connor knew it would take a long time to get through the red tape at the border. They didn't have time for delays, but what other choice did they have? They would get into even more trouble if they tried to sneak into the United States.

"What can we do?" Pedro asked.

"We were wondering if you could give us information about the man in charge at the factory," Connor said.

"What did he look like?" Pedro asked.

When Connor described him, Pedro's expression went from cautious to troubled. "This man, he had scars?" He brushed at his cheeks. "Here?"

"That's right," Brooke said.

Pedro murmured something to his wife, and she gasped.

"We know this man," Pedro told them. "Arturo Sanchez. He is not good."

"What do you mean?" Connor asked. "Is he part of a drug cartel or the mob or something like that?"

"That I do not know," Pedro said. "It is possible. He is the richest man in Ejido Ojo de Agua. He owns many food stands all over this part of Mexico. But he is—what is the word? Cruel. To his employees and to his family. You do not want his attention."

Brooke sucked in a loud breath, her outrage apparent. "Why doesn't his wife leave him or turn him in to the police?"

"This is not America. The police will do nothing against Arturo Sanchez. If they do, they might end up . . ." Pedro put his finger to his throat and made a slicing motion. "Some already have."

At the confirmation of her worst fears, Brooke felt dizzy. She and Connor had escaped the factory in the nick of time. She didn't even want to think about what a man like that would do to a couple of trespassers on his property.

There was a definite connection between Skytech 1 and Tecnología del Cielo. Jordan and Derek were dead, and a Mexican man with a reputation for killing people was somehow involved. But how? Arturo Sanchez must have a partner inside Skytech 1. Jordan had found out about the connection and probably Derek had as well. But there were three more men besides Brooke working on that project. One might be a murderer.

"Were you followed here?" Caution crept over Pedro's features.

Brooke understood the man's concern. If Sanchez was as ruthless as Pedro claimed—and she had no trouble believing him—Pedro and Consuela would be putting themselves in danger if they were discovered harboring Connor and Brooke, even for a short time.

"No, and we didn't mention you," Connor assured the man. "He doesn't know we're acquainted at all."

Pedro nodded. "What else can we do for you?"

"You've been a big help," Connor said. "Now we need to get home before anyone else is killed."

Consuela jumped up and bustled behind the curtain. She returned a few moments later with a paper bag.

Brooke accepted the bag, then peeked inside to find corn tortillas and bottles of water. She was touched by the woman's generosity. "Gracias."

Consuela nodded.

"We'd better go," Connor said, standing up.

Brooke got to her feet and grabbed the bag. "How can we thank you?" she asked the Molinas.

"Someday maybe you come back and stay in our hotel." Pedro stood next to his wife. "When it is safer, sí?"

Brooke somehow managed a smile. "Sí."

Pedro handed Connor a few bills. "For your trip home."

"No, I can't accept this," Connor told him.

"Please," Pedro said. "You might need it."

"I will pay you back," Connor promised him. "As soon as we get home, I'll wire the money."

Pedro examined him, then nodded. "I believe you will. But first you must get there."

Connor clasped Pedro's hand. "Thank you, my friend."

"*Vaya con Dios*," Pedro said. "Go with God, mi amigo, and I hope to see you again in better times."

Connor put his arm around Brooke's shoulders and ushered her out of the hotel. They hurried to his car and got inside.

He wasted no time in leaving. He started the car, and the engine rumbled to life.

As they drove, Connor remarked, "Our border crossing won't be nearly as easy as the one coming in."

"I hope we're not delayed too long." Brooke winced, and panic clutched at her throat. "Or worse." Her voice wavered with tears. "What if we're arrested?"

"We won't get arrested," Connor said. "Trust me."

Though their relationship had started off on shaky ground, he'd proven himself in a thousand ways since then. He'd gotten them out of the closet, hadn't he? And off the roof.

Brooke reached over and grabbed his hand, holding it tightly. "I do."

When Brooke and Connor arrived at the border inspection station, the barest evidence of sunrise glowed along the eastern horizon, where the blackness of night gave way to a faint purple glow. Brooke judged dawn to be about an hour or so away, which put the time at roughly 5:00 a.m.

Once again, they joined a short line of cars and waited.

When a border patrol agent approached the car, he asked for their passports.

"They were stolen," Connor said.

"Any other forms of ID?" the man asked.

"Unfortunately, no," Connor replied, then began to explain the situation.

The agent stopped him. "Please pull over to the side so we can verify your identities."

Connor did as instructed, then turned to Brooke. "What was in the bag Consuela gave you?"

She reached inside and removed two bottles of water. After handing one to him, she said, "And corn tortillas."

"Thanks," he said. "I'll have a tortilla later if we're still waiting."

"I'm not hungry either." Her stomach was in knots, and she couldn't imagine eating right now. She took the other bottle of water and drank it.

Soon the agent returned to their car and tapped on the window.

Connor rolled his window down.

"Come with me," the agent said. He led them into the building and down a short corridor.

Brooke and Connor entered a room that strongly reminded her of the one in Los Angeles where she'd been questioned after Jordan's death.

They'd no sooner seated themselves in two hard chairs when a woman wearing a uniform entered. She tossed a notepad and a pen on the table and sat across from them. "I hear your passports were stolen," she said without preamble.

"Yes," Connor said.

"What happened?" the woman asked.

"We ran into some trouble in Mexico," Brooke replied.

The woman cocked her head. "What were you doing in Mexico?"

Brooke hesitated. Where to begin?

But Connor spoke before she could gather her thoughts. "I'm a newspaper journalist, and I'm researching a story about tourism in Mexico."

With an effort, Brooke managed to keep her surprise hidden.

"Are you now?" the woman asked, then faced Brooke. "And what are you doing here?"

Brooke bit her lip, grasping for an answer. She grabbed Connor's hand and said, "Moral support."

He squeezed her fingers. "If you don't believe me, call Steven Fitzsimmons. He's the deputy managing editor."

"I'll do that," the woman said. "In a while. First, I want to know more about this trouble you ran into."

Brooke gritted her teeth, frustrated. They didn't have time to sit here answering questions. Two men had been killed already. They needed to get back to LA with everything they'd learned. "Aren't we allowed to make a phone call or something?" Impatience made her voice tight.

"You're not under arrest," the woman said. "We'll let him call his editor in a bit."

"Please call Detective Travis of the LA Police Department," Brooke insisted. "He's in the homicide division. Tell him we're here."

The woman appraised her. Then she slid the pen and notepad across the table toward them. "Give me your names. I'll make the call."

When she'd gone, Brooke turned toward Connor. "You lied."

"Who, me?" he asked innocently.

"You said you were writing an article about tourism in Mexico. But you told me you never lie."

"That wasn't a lie." He smiled. "I will write that article."

Connor paced the perimeter of the room, antsy to get back to LA. He'd spent far more time locked in windowless rooms than he had patience for. At least this one was bigger than the closet in Mexico.

"How long do you think we've been here?" Brooke asked.

She sat at the table, her expression calmer than he could manage. Her hair hung in tangled locks, and dark smudges marred the skin beneath her eyes.

She was the most beautiful woman he'd ever seen.

"Close to an hour, I'd say." He scrubbed his fingers across his scalp. "What's taking them so long?"

Before she could answer, the door opened. The agent who'd questioned them earlier entered. "I spoke to Detective Travis and Steven Fitzsimmons. You're both free to go, but you need to stop at the desk and sign some paperwork."

"Thank you," Brooke said as she leaped to her feet.

The woman ushered them down the hallway and directed them to the desk.

After Connor and Brooke signed the paperwork, they rushed out to his car. He opened the door for her, then slid behind the wheel and drove away.

Traffic was light, and for a moment Connor wondered at the fact. Then he counted the days and realized with a start that today was Sunday. Only yesterday they'd driven to Mexico, but it felt like a lifetime.

Brooke's phone rang. She checked the screen. "It's Travis."

"You'd better answer," Connor suggested.

Brooke picked up. "We already left. Let me put you on speakerphone, so you can talk to Connor too."

"Okay," the detective said. "Talk."

Brooke had the most at stake. She was the one who'd been accused of murdering her boss. Connor motioned for her to begin.

Brooke spelled out the entire story in a logical progression of the facts. She laid out their dramatic escapades calmly and concisely, as if giving the results of one of her programming tests rather than an international adventure that belonged in a movie.

"Let me get this straight," Travis said when she had finished speaking. "You two crossed the southern border, tracked down a manufacturing plant that mirrors the one at Skytech 1, and escaped capture by a group of armed men?" Incredulity colored his voice. "You're both insane."

"You're absolutely right," Brooke agreed with obvious exhaustion.

"No, we did what we had to do when we were ignored by the authorities," Connor interjected. "Brooke told you about that file being tampered with. You didn't do anything about it, and another man died. What were we supposed to do? Wait around for you to decide to listen? How many more people would have died if we had?"

"Do you think I've been sitting on my hands this whole time?" Travis asked. "I have two murders on my hands. I've been investigating the—" He stopped. "I'm not going to explain my actions to you two. Now give me the name of that company again."

"Tecnología del Cielo," Brooke said. "It means Technology of the Sky."

"Let me search for it," Travis said. A few moments later, he continued, "I didn't find anything. Unfortunately, Mexican business records are not a matter of public record in the States. I'm going to have to unravel a tangle of red tape to discover the name of the American business partner." He sighed, as if it were their fault. "I hate red tape."

Connor didn't blame him. A journalist encountered tons of red tape every day. It was part of the job.

"What are you going to do with us?" Brooke asked, her voice trembling.

The detective was silent for a couple of beats. "I could order you to come downtown and subject you to hours of questioning until you detail every minute that has passed from the last time I saw you until now. But I don't have time for that. You're going to go home. On the condition that the two of you write out a detailed report of everything you know and how you know it."

"We will," Connor assured him.

"And don't do anything stupid," Travis added. "I'm going to keep an eye on both of you."

When Brooke and Connor arrived at her house, she couldn't help but breathe a relieved sigh. It seemed like she'd been gone for years.

As she exited the car, the morning sun beat down on her from the east, and she lifted her face toward it, eyes closed. "It feels so good to be home."

"And free," Connor added as he got out and stood next to her.

Brooke nodded. "I need a shower and clean clothes and about twelve hours of sleep."

"Me too. But now comes the hard part." Connor frowned. "We have to wait for Travis to do the research on Tecnología del Cielo." The phrase rolled off his lips so easily he sounded like a native Spanish speaker.

She grinned at him. "Maybe not."

"You have a plan?" He raised his eyebrows. "One that supersedes a shower?"

"Maybe not supersedes," Brooke admitted, "but I do have a plan. Mexican business records might not be a matter of public record, but many American records are."

"Meaning?"

"I know the names of all the Skytech 1 employees who had anything to do with the ten-drive stripe storage array project. And I know my way around a computer. I'll bet I can uncover documentation to tie someone to the Mexican company—tax records, travel records, something."

Admiration shone on his face, and she couldn't help feeling pleased.

"Do you mind if I stick around and watch the master at work?" Connor asked.

A pleasant tickle zipped down her spine. Truth be told, she'd dreaded the moment when he left. The last twenty-four hours had been harrowing and horrible, but she hated to see their partnership end.

"You can stay," she told him. "After all, somebody has to feed the cat while I clean up."

Connor grinned. "Deal."

Together they walked up the sidewalk to her front door. Exhaustion tugged at her heavy limbs as she inserted the key into the lock. If not for Connor's presence, she would probably fall into bed and sleep for a week. But there was important research to be done.

Brooke unlocked the knob and the dead bolt and pushed the door inward.

"Sammy," she called as she stepped inside, "we're home!"

But it was not Sammy who welcomed her.

Greg Flynn, her coworker at Skytech 1, stood in the center of her living room. He held a gun, and it was pointed directly at her.

21

"It was you?" Brooke asked, trembling. The past day had scraped her emotions raw, and she was more exhausted than she'd ever been in her life. Tears hovered just below the surface, and the only thing holding them back was a rising panic when she realized she was once again staring down the barrel of a gun. "You killed Jordan?"

Greg noticed Connor behind her. "Get in here, and close the door."

Connor did as he was told and stepped next to Brooke.

How she wished she could clutch his hand and draw strength from the contact. But she didn't dare move.

An angry yowl drifted down the hallway. She noticed Greg's bloody arms, which bore the evidence of an encounter with Sammy. Good for him.

"You won't get away with this," Connor told Greg. "Even if you manage to escape the police here, those guys in Mexico will flip on you."

Greg laughed. "Yeah, I heard you met one of my partners." He smirked at Brooke. "Arturo called when he found your employee ID."

So that was why they hadn't been killed outright. Sanchez needed to contact his American partner first.

"He's not a nice guy," Brooke said. "Why did you pick someone like that to work with?"

"We didn't need nice," Greg replied. "We needed investors and cheap labor."

"We?" Connor asked.

"My partner." Greg smiled. "Derek."

Brooke's jaw went slack. "But you and Derek didn't even like each other."

His smile widened. "We were roommates at MIT, and he was my best friend for years."

A snort blasted from Connor. "Yet you killed him."

Greg shrugged, his expression nonchalant. "It was out of necessity."

Too many new thoughts whirled in her tired brain. Derek and Greg were friends? Greg murdered him? She pressed her fingers against her temples and tried to clear her head. "I don't understand. Why did you kill Jordan?"

Greg was silent for a moment. "It won't hurt to tell you. I mean, you're not going to be telling anyone else. Either of you."

The implication sent a shiver of fear down her spine.

"Like I said, Derek and I were roommates. Before graduation we heard about Skytech 1's plans to create a state-of-the-art storage array that would revolutionize the way data is stored and accessed on the Internet." Passion flared in his eyes. "Do you know how cool that is? We wanted to be a part of it. But as we talked it out, we realized we didn't merely want to work on the project. We wanted to own it. Think of the money. We could become billionaires."

Brooke could feel the disgust radiating from Connor's rigid stance. "But the idea, the project—they weren't yours," she said.

"But they could be," Greg insisted. "We were smart enough. We sketched out a plan together. First, we had to get hired onto the project. That part was easy. We researched Jordan's and Ed's hiring history so we knew exactly what would appeal to them, then made sure our résumés highlighted enough of our experience and expertise to get us an interview."

Their plan had worked. They'd been hired within a few months of each other at the beginning of the project.

"You pretended to be competing with each other, but you were actually working together all along," Brooke said. "Why?"

"We didn't want anyone to think we were partners in anything," Greg answered. "Then they might look too closely at our work together."

Grudgingly, she had to admit the logic made sense. And something else made sense too.

"You stole data about the project a little at a time. You siphoned critical files from Skytech 1's system."

Greg sneered at Connor. "She's smart, if a little slow."

A murderer insulting her intelligence? The comment rankled, and Brooke gritted her teeth. From the corner of her eye she saw Connor clench his fists.

"So you and Derek stole the project out from under Skytech 1's nose," Connor said. "You found investors in Mexico and built a mirror manufacturing plant based on Skytech 1's blueprints."

"Regulations on technology companies south of the border are far less rigid than here in the States," Greg said.

"So why blow the test?" she asked. "You had everything you needed already. Why not move to Mexico and get to work?"

"You saw the facility down there. It won't be ready for a few more weeks. Besides, I don't want to compete with Skytech 1. I want to get a jump on them. I want to be the first to market with that storage array."

Brooke realized their plan was pretty smart. Despicable, of course, but it could have worked. Except for one thing. "Jordan found out," she said. "That's why you killed him."

"That's where Derek bungled the plan," Greg said. "We've been e-mailing files to ourselves for years, maintaining a progressive record of the project's development. Never enough data or often enough to trigger Skytech 1's security filters."

Again, a smart plan. Brooke had e-mailed herself a file so she could work on it at home, and it hadn't raised any questions.

"But Derek got sloppy," Greg went on. "When we bombed the system test, he forgot to destroy the off-site backups."

"Off-site backups?" Connor asked.

"Skytech 1 keeps a backup of their entire system in a facility in Kansas in case of a physical disaster here in LA," Brooke explained. "Jordan must have gotten suspicious when the test failed. When he couldn't find anything in the current files, he checked the off-site backup and traced the data thefts."

"And there you were, ready to take the fall for his murder," Greg said smugly.

Brooke wanted to slap that arrogant smirk off his face. But there was the small matter of a gun pointed directly at her chest. Her throat tightened. They had to do something, but what? She had to keep him talking.

Every muscle in Connor's body was taut. The guy in front of him was a thief and a cold-blooded murderer. Greg had killed not once but twice. And now he intended to carve two more notches in his bloody belt.

Beside him, Brooke appeared outwardly calm, but her tight voice betrayed the strain she had to be feeling. "Why did you frame me?" she asked. "I've never done anything to you or Derek."

"I didn't choose you because of some sort of vendetta," Greg responded. "You were merely a matter of convenience. Everybody knows you get to work at least an hour before anyone else. And carrying a purse like yours would immediately send people's suspicions in the direction of a female. Plus, you're tall for a woman, almost as tall as the rest of us. Any number of people could pass for you as long as the camera didn't show you too closely."

A sour taste invaded Connor's mouth. "So you put on a UCLA jacket, bought a purse, and made a copy of her security card."

Greg laughed. "It was the easiest system I've ever hacked. Pretty pathetic for a technology company."

Brooke wavered on her feet.

Connor reached out a steadying hand, almost expecting the killer to stop them from touching each other.

"You seem tired, Brooke." False concern rang sarcastically in Greg's voice. "Don't worry. You'll get to sleep. A long, deep sleep that lasts forever."

Connor's stomach tightened. "Like your buddy?" he snapped.

This guy wasn't bluffing. Unless Connor did something soon, both Brooke and he were going to end up in the morgue. His mind skipped around, searching for a way out. But this was not a locked door. There was no AC vent to climb through, no rooftop to escape from. All that would get them out of here was blunt force. At least this time there was only one gun, not five.

"Exactly like Derek," Greg said, shaking his head in mock sorrow.

"Why did you kill him?" Brooke asked.

"Poor Derek. He got squeamish when the cops started crawling all over the place. Started to lose his nerve." Greg grinned at Brooke, as if they were sharing a private joke. "He even thought you were catching on to us and came over here to question you, to see what you knew, even though I warned him to stay away. He was about to blow the whole plan. I couldn't let that happen."

Something Detective Travis told them surfaced from memory.

"Criminals always turn on each other when things get hot," Connor told him. "You're as predictable as the next scumbag."

Greg went white with fury, and he swung the gun from Brooke to Connor.

With a silent sigh of relief, Connor released her arm and took a step away from her. He wanted Greg to point the weapon at him, not her.

"What a shame," Brooke remarked. She actually sounded sorrowful, like she pitied the guy or something.

Greg aimed the gun at her.

"You had so much going for you," she continued. "You're smart and ambitious. What have you done?"

Greg snorted. "Are you serious?" He raised both hands in a gesture of disbelief. For a fraction of a second, the gun wasn't pointed at either of them.

Acting on instinct, Connor charged. He lowered his head like a bull and barreled into the soft flesh of Greg's stomach.

The gun went off as Connor tackled him to the floor. They landed hard.

Connor planted a knee on Greg's chest and grappled for the gun. *Got it!* He moved to toss it to Brooke—

Her limp body slid down the wall to the floor, leaving a trail of blood behind.

"Brooke!" Her name ripped from Connor's throat. He launched himself off Greg—who rolled to his side, gasping—and stumbled to her prone body.

With a loud *crack*, the front door burst open.

Connor was dimly aware of a parade of police officers in blue uniforms rushing into the room. On his knees, he reached out to pull Brooke up but stopped. Blood seeped from a bullet-sized hole in the right side of her shirt. His heart thundering like a drum in his ears, he placed two fingers on her throat and almost fainted with relief when he felt a pulse.

"Get back. Let us help." Detective Travis stood over Connor, his normally stern countenance full of concern.

Without a word, Connor sank onto the floor.

Travis dropped onto his knees and took Brooke's wrist as a female officer rushed forward to examine the wound.

Connor couldn't tear his gaze from Brooke's face—the pale skin, the delicate features, a few faint freckles on her nose he hadn't noticed before. What had he done? He'd never forgive himself for hurting her.

Travis sat back on his heels. "It's a flesh wound. She'll be fine."

As if to prove his point, Brooke's eyelids fluttered open. Her voice, though weak, held the bite of sarcasm. "I'm touched by your concern."

Connor felt light-headed. She was okay.

"You're tougher than you look," the detective said, then went on in a kinder voice. "Lie still. The ambulance will be here in a minute."

The sound of a distant siren seeped through the open doorway.

Behind Connor, two officers hauled Greg to his feet, his hands cuffed behind his back, and marched him outside.

When they were out of sight, Travis rounded on Connor. "Just what did you think you were doing?"

"I—" Connor scrubbed a hand across his mouth. "I don't know." Then a thought occurred to him. "How do you know what I did? Were you watching?"

"Of course we were," the detective snapped and pointed at the curtains.

They were parted about three inches. The hems were ragged and frayed, apparently the victim of a vindictive cat who didn't appreciate being left alone for more than a day. Sammy's angry attack must have slid them open, therefore providing the perfect peephole from which Travis could watch the entire scene play out.

"I told you I was going to keep an eye on both of you," Travis reminded him. Then his lips twitched with humor. "Besides, sometimes people need more than moral support."

Brooke refused to let the EMTs carry her out to the ambulance on a stretcher. "I'm perfectly capable of walking," she told them.

"Please let us assist you," one of the paramedics urged.

Detective Travis had called it a flesh wound, but the pain shafting through her body almost convinced her otherwise. Finally, she gave in and allowed the paramedics to help her onto the stretcher.

They strapped her onto the stretcher, and four EMTs, one at each corner, rolled her out of the house.

The sun shone in a blue sky, a perfect California day. It didn't seem possible that a murderer had recently broken into her house and attempted to kill her and Connor.

After the paramedics carried her down the porch stairs, Connor rushed to her side and grabbed her hand. "I'll check on Sammy and then come to the hospital."

"Thanks," Brooke said. "I'm glad he likes you."

"He's an excellent judge of character," he reminded her with a grin. Then he sobered. "I'm so sorry about this."

"I'm okay," Brooke said, waving off his apology. "Don't worry about it."

Connor looked like he wanted to say something else, but he didn't. He simply squeezed her hand.

When they were ready to load her into the ambulance, she clung to his hand, reluctant to let him go.

Brooke settled back against the pillows in the hospital bed. She'd been examined and x-rayed, and the doctor had confirmed that the gunshot was only a flesh wound. He had given Brooke pain medication and recommended that she stay in the hospital overnight for observation.

A nurse poked her head into the room. "You have a visitor. Should I send him in?"

Brooke hoped it was Connor. "Yes, please."

Connor strolled into the room with a large bouquet of flowers. "How are you feeling?"

She smiled, so glad to see him again. "I'm all right." She told him what the doctor had said.

"Good." He approached her and set the vase on the night table.

Brooke admired the bouquet. "The flowers are beautiful. Thank you."

"You're welcome," Connor said. "I'm sorry I didn't get here sooner, but I stopped to wire money to Pedro first. I wanted to pay him back immediately."

"That was thoughtful of you," she said.

"I made sure Sammy had enough to eat and drink. He's doing fine."

"Did he destroy anything?" Brooke asked.

"The curtains took the brunt of his wrath," Connor answered.

She laughed. "I was afraid of that."

He sat down in the chair next to her bed. "I talked to Holly.

She was really sorry about what happened to you."

"I hope she can find closure now that she knows who killed Jordan," Brooke said.

"Me too," Connor said. "She plans to visit you when you get home. And she's bringing her daughter."

She smiled at the thought. "That sounds nice."

"I also talked to Detective Travis," he said.

"What did he say?" Brooke asked.

"As we expected, Greg is going to be locked up for a long time," Connor said. "And they're investigating the factory in Mexico."

She recalled the recent events and the shocking revelations, and she still found it hard to believe. "I'm so glad it's over."

"I can't tell you how sorry I am," Connor said, taking her hand. "I could have gotten you killed."

"Like a million times in the past few days." She attempted a weak laugh, but it hurt so much she abandoned the idea. "See what depending on a guy got me?"

He didn't respond, but tears filled his eyes.

"Hey." Brooke brushed at his cheek, enjoying the feel of his warm skin beneath her fingers. "That was a bad joke. You saved my life. If not for you, Greg would have killed us both for sure. You're my hero."

The statement hung in the air between them.

Realization crept over her, stronger than the pain, and she marveled at the revelation. Connor *was* her hero. Not the kind in books or movies but a real man, one who had earned her respect. Brooke didn't want him to disappear from her life. She was finally ready to take a chance and trust him completely.

She grinned. "I guess you got your story, huh?"

Connor raised his other hand and gently tucked her hair behind her ears. His fingers trailed down to her lips. Then he leaned close to her and said in a husky voice, "I hope I've got more than that."

When his lips touched hers, Brooke knew he had far more than a story.

He had won her heart.

Up to this point, we've been doing all the writing. Now it's *your* turn!

Tell us what you think about this book, the characters, the bad guy, or anything else you'd like to share with us about this series. We can't wait to hear from *you*!

Log on to give us your feedback at:
https://www.surveymonkey.com/r/sweetintrigue

Annie's® FICTION

Learn more about Annie's fiction books at

AnniesFiction.com

We've designed the Annie's Fiction website especially for you!

Access your e-books and audiobooks • Manage your account

Choose from one of these great series:

Amish Inn Mysteries	Chocolate Shoppe Mysteries
Annie's Attic Mysteries	Creative Woman Mysteries
Annie's Mysteries Unraveled	Hearts of Amish Country
Annie's Quilted Mysteries	Inn at Magnolia Harbor
Annie's Secrets of the Quilt	Secrets of the Castleton Manor Library
Annie's Sweet Intrigue	Scottish Bakehouse Mysteries
Antique Shop Mysteries	Victorian Mansion Flower Shop Mysteries

What are you waiting for? Visit us now at **AnniesFiction.com!**